Unfr

Valos of Sonhadra, Volume 9

Regine Abel

Published by Regine Abel.

Copyright © 2018

Copyright

All rights reserved. The unauthorized reproduction or distribution of this copyrighted work is illegal and punishable by law. No part of this book may be used or reproduced electronically or in print without written permission of the author, except in the case of brief quotations embodied in reviews.

This book uses mature language and explicit sexual content. It is not intended for anyone under the age of 18.

This book is a work of fiction. Names, characters, places, and incidents are either products of the author's imagination or are used fictitiously. Any resemblance to actual persons, living or dead, events, or locales is entirely coincidental.

Dedication

MUCH LOVE TO ALL THE wonderful ladies of the Valos of Sonhadra series. Thank you for all the support, creativity, laughter, silliness, and all the other good stuff in between. I can't remember ever having so much fun doing a collaborative project.

Nero, you're the best shoulder a girl could ever need when writer's block and self-doubt kicks her in the teeth. Keep on having those crazy dreams!

Mom and Dad, I praise God every day that I should have been so blessed with such supportive and loving parents. Because of you, no mountain is too high, no challenge is too great. Thank you for always being there for me, whatever my endeavors, for believing in me, and going out of your way to help me live my dreams, however wild and crazy they may be.

I love you.

Valos of Sonhadra Series

WHEN AN ORBITAL PRISON is torn through a wormhole and crashes on an unknown planet, it's every woman for herself to escape the wreckage. As though savage beasts and harsh, alien climates aren't enough, the survivors discover the world isn't uninhabited, and must face new challenges—risking not only their lives, but their hearts.

Welcome to Sonhadra.

The Valos of Sonhadra series is the shared vision of nine sci-fi and fantasy romance authors. Each book is a standalone, containing its own Happy Ever After, and can be read in any order.

Unfrozen

WHEN THE PENITENTIARY ship she's incarcerated in gets sucked into an anomaly, Lydia barely survives the crash onto an alien planet. Only the sadistic experiments performed on her by the prison's scientist allow her to survive this harsh and dangerous world. The future looks grim until she stumbles upon a magnificent city of ice and its most unusual inhabitant.

Kai is fascinated by the delicate stranger fallen from the stars with the power to bring his hibernating city back to life. She stirs emotions long forgotten by his frozen heartstone. Can she be the salvation of his people or will the trap set by the Creators bring about their collective doom?

Chapter 1

LYDIA

The long, tortured scream of Prisoner 2098 ended on a choking, gurgling sound before rising again with renewed agony. Sitting on the frozen floor of my holding cell, my knees hugged to my chest, I rocked back and forth as another wail assaulted my ears through the door. The scientists had been working on Quinn—my sister in pain—far longer than usual today.

Once done with her, they would come for me.

My stomach churned; the coils of dread overtaking the pangs of hunger. Dr. Sobin never fed me before an experiment. She wouldn't want me puking all over her or choking on my own vomit. At that point, I'd welcome that death over what awaited me.

Another hot flash set me on fire. Beads of sweat erupted over my bare skin. I unfolded my legs and leaned my bare back against the cold metal wall behind me. Arms stretched, legs spread, I waited for my body to cool down. Even though I wasn't going through menopause, at twenty-four, the constant hell of its worst manifestation had made me its bitch. Growing up, physicians had failed to explain my condition.

Since my arrival on the space penitentiary, the *Concord*, Dr. Sobin's experiments had only increased the symptoms. On a good day, I'd only burn up five or six times per hour. Lately, it felt more like once every five minutes. Although I could regulate my temperature, doing so expended a lot of energy and left me famished. Starved as I was, my only remaining option was to ride it out.

With my average body temperature of forty-two degrees Celsius, well above safe levels for a human adult, the prison guards kept me by myself in this cold room. It suited me fine since most of the inmates on this prison ship were deviant freaks; the worst criminals from Earth, condemned for life.

For a short while, I'd begun forming a friendship with three other inmates, Quinn, Zoya and Preta—the rare decent people in this hellhole. One by one, they'd been taken away to be experimented on as well. I had no idea what became of Zoya and Preta. Quinn, I could hear…

I heaved a sigh of relief as the hot flash faded, the sound echoing loudly in the otherwise deafening silence.

Silence?

Oh God!

A whimper escaped me, and I hugged my knees to my chest again. Rocking back and forth with greater intensity, my back thudded against the wall with each backward motion.

They're coming for me… They're coming for me!

Bile rose in my throat and a shudder of fear coursed through me. My gaze fell on the patient tunic still neatly folded on my cot propped against the wall across from me. I crawled over and slipped the tunic on. Sobin wanted me naked for her twisted experiments but forcing them to strip it off me would delay my torture by a few more seconds. When you had no hope left, every little mercy counted.

My stomach clenched and my nails dug into my calves when the deactivation beep of my cell's security lock resounded. Gaze flicking around the white room like a trapped animal, I looked in vain for a place to hide. God only knew why I did that, every single time. Besides a sink, a toilet, and a small shelf, the room lay completely barren.

The door slid open with a faint swish, letting in the scent of antiseptics and chemicals. The glaring light from the lab stabbed my eyes. I flinched and squinted as Jonah's bulky silhouette stepped in. Scratching his blossoming beer gut through his grey prison guard uniform, he stopped inches from my bare feet. His pale, baby-blue eyes promised a world of pain if I made any kind of a fuss.

How could anyone with such pretty eyes be so cruel?

I swallowed past the lump in my throat and willed myself to get up, to accept the inevitable. I knew better than to give him any excuse to brutalize me...

He'll get me anyway...

And yet, as soon as he reached a hand toward me, my sanity snapped.

Stomach roiling with pure terror, I screamed and scrambled away from him. Begging... Pleading... He grabbed my wrist in a bruising hold and yanked me forward. I struggled, the need to flee overriding any logical thought. My skin flared, burning so hot that my tunic blackened. The scent of scorched fabric and plastic stung my nose.

Despite his protective glove, Jonah yelped and released me. I fell, my hip striking the hard floor with a violent thud. Pain radiated down my leg as I scrambled back, but I ignored it, my focus on one thing: getting away from him. He shook his hand before looking at his gloved palm as if expecting it to be on fire.

"You fucking bitch," Jonah hissed, pulling his shock-baton from his belt.

"I… I'm so…sorry… I'm sorry… Please!"

I pressed myself against the wall, wishing it would swallow me whole. With morbid fascination, I watched the light blue head of the dark stick close in on my exposed skin.

Lightning struck.

My muscles tensed to breaking, followed by spasms that clawed at every nerve ending. Vision blurred, I lay helpless on the floor, my limbs flopping like a fish out of water. As the tremors subsided, a cool metal collar clasped around my neck.

"Get up, you stupid cunt, before I stick my boots in your ribs."

Jonah yanked on the pole attached to my collar, the hard metal edge chafing the skin of my neck. Dizzy and further weakened by the energy expended in my flare-up, I struggled to get back up on my feet. Dragging me after him, he led me like a rabid dog on a catch stick to the operating table in the center of the lab. I followed on wobbly legs, my hands clasped around the stick to prevent it from jerking my neck too hard.

Dr. Sobin watched us approach with an annoyed expression on her long, horsey face. She stood on the other side of the operating table next to her assistant Lucinda, ironically nicknamed Lucky. Behind them, a few shelves were embedded between the sets of white counters that ran the length of the light-grey wall. Their glass doors hid nothing of their contents; countless vials and a bunch of jars filled with unidentified organs floating in liquid.

Lips pinched in displeasure, the doctor gestured with her head for Lucky to assist Jonah in getting me ready for the procedure.

"We have too much important work to do, 2012, for you to be wasting our time with your childish tantrums," Sobin said.

May you burn in Hell...

The crazy bitch didn't seem to understand that I never agreed to be her guinea pig. But then again, I wasn't a person to her. I was Prisoner 2012, a number, a tool for her science project.

Jonah held me still in front of the operating table. Lucky circled around it to rid me of my burned tunic. I didn't fight, feeling both drained and numb. Her dark eyes peered at me with compassion as she removed the ruined fabric covering me. I wanted to claw at her face and tell her where she could shove her sympathy. Rumor had it that, like me, she'd been brought here against her will, under false pretenses and coerced into collaborating with Sobin. Yet, I felt none of the kinship with her that I did with Quinn, Zoya and Preta. Victim or not, Lucinda helped them hurt me. For that alone, I hated her.

Jonah jerked the stick forward, causing more lancing pain in my neck. I couldn't even turn to glare at him.

"Get on," he snapped.

"We don't have all day," Dr. Sobin added.

I half-climbed, half-flopped onto the cold, hard surface. Jonah released my neck from the collar but held the shock-stick near my face, in case I got any funny ideas. I didn't even get a chance to rub the raw skin of my neck before Lucky strapped my wrists to the table. Fear crept back in as Dr. Sobin placed neural nodes on my body and her assistant picked up a huge syringe, the type normally used for spinal taps.

Tears pricked my eyes and my lips quivered.

"Now, now," Dr. Sobin said, as if addressing a misbehaving child, "there's no reason for that. Today should be the consecration of all our hard work."

She stuck the last node on my leg then checked my vitals. The beep of my erratic heartbeat sounded like the warning chime of a ticking bomb about to go off.

"Dr. Craig achieved total success with her experiment on 2098 today. She left us this wondrous serum, the missing ingredient for our own project. So, you be a good girl and don't deny us a similar success."

Us?

Who the hell was 'us' anyway? I could never tell if the crazy woman was using the royal *we* or if she genuinely thought we were all in this together.

"Lucky, if you would do the honors," she said, stepping aside so her assistant could approach me.

A heavy weight seemed to settle on my chest, choking the air out of my lungs. My pulse raced with accrued intensity while Lucky disinfected the skin in the crease of my elbow. I whimpered and strained against my restraints. The assistant gave me an apologetic look before sticking a needle port in my arm. Picking up the giant needle she'd been fiddling with previously, she turned back to me and approached its tip to the insertion point of the port.

My ragged breathing echoed loudly in my ears as I stared at the fiery red liquid in the giant needle. It was supposed to be a mix of Sobin's mad scientist concoction and a healing serum derived from Quinn's samples. Combined, Sobin believed it would turn me into a human torch. At the snail pace it had to be administered to me, I never understood why they didn't simply use a drip.

Lucky slowly pressed the plunger. Searing agony radiated through my arm as the first drops entered my system. It felt like acid burning my flesh, consuming me from within. I shrieked, my body writhing against the straps holding me down.

A deafening boom drowned out the scream tearing from my vocal cords.

The room lurched. The needle, still ninety percent full, tore out of the port with a stabbing pain as Lucky stumbled back. Through blurred vision, I watched Lucky and Dr. Sobin crash against the wall while fire continued to course through my veins like molten lava devouring everything in its path. They yelped, looking for something to hold on to. The room pitched again, tossing my persecutors around. Even while holding me securely to the table, the straps bit into my flesh.

Despite the pain fogging my mind, I realized something terrible was happening to the ship.

Are we under attack? Did we hit something?

The alarm blared as Dr. Sobin and Jonah shouted words I couldn't process.

Another violent tilt sent my tormentors flying through the room. Lucky screeched. I couldn't see what had happened to her and didn't really care. Her gut-wrenching screams mingled with mine when another wave of agony speared through me. Objects toppled to the floor in a cacophony of broken glass as the prison ship rocked as if tumbling in a free fall.

We're going to die...

The violent tremors rattled the teeth in my head. Searing pain shredded my spine to pieces and I knew no more.

I REGAINED CONSCIOUSNESS, coughing the acrid stench of smoke as it burnt my lungs. More screams pierced my ears, but not Lucky's this time. Dried tears—or God only knew what else—glued my eyes shut. I pried them open and they watered, stinging from the smoke.

Biting back a moan as my battered body complained, I turned my sore neck in the direction of the tortured wails. Chaos reigned in the room. Bent and broken walls revealed the bare skeleton of the ship. Dr. Sobin lay on the floor with both of her legs shattered, the bones protruding through the blood-soaked, ripped fabric of her green scrubs. She clawed at the debris littered floor to crawl away from the still form of a body engulfed in flames. Lucky's, I assumed. The fire, spreading quickly, was already climbing the doctor's scrubs and licking at my operating table.

Sobin's not getting away.

Poetic justice if there ever was.

I couldn't dwell on the doctor's fate, however. Despite my heightened resistance to extreme temperatures—both warm and cold—sitting in an open fire would kill me. And so would inhaling too much smoke.

Half of the straps shackling me to the operating table had been torn off. Through another bout of coughing, I unstrapped the remaining ones with my free hand. The vivid marks the restraints had left on my skin made me cringe. I rolled off the table, grinding my teeth through the painful sting of blood rushing back to my extremities, and tried to block out Dr. Sobin's gurgling howls. Willing my stiff muscles to cooperate, I tiptoed through the broken glass and toppled vials.

Vials containing what? Damn it...

I needed to cover my feet—the rest of me too, while at it—because God only knew what kind of twisted things those vials contained and what they'd do to me once they entered my bloodstream.

Not to mention if I inhale too much of it.

Coughing and wheezing, I limped toward the lab's door. Along the way, I snagged a laser scalpel amidst the debris and a clean surgery blanket which I pressed to my nose to breathe through. The lab's door stood partially open. The motion detector didn't respond to my approach. Not surprising. Tapping the opening switch on the wall didn't help either.

As I turned sideways to squeeze through, my gaze snagged on Jonah crumpled in the corner of the room, his neck set at an odd angle. I contemplated going to him to grab his shock-baton. However, in my current state, I wouldn't have the energy to move his massive body to retrieve it from underneath him. Sucking in my gut—not like I had any—I slipped through the opening, my butt and breasts scraping against the wall.

My jaw dropped as I took in the extent of the devastation of our pod. Large sections of wall had been torn off and entire cells were missing. This had not been some ship malfunction. We had crashed.

Did Quinn make it? Had Zoya and Preta also been in our pod?

An explosion from the lab snapped me out of my daze and spurred me to get out through the gaping hole in the outer wall. I stumbled outside. The warm rays of the sun and a gentle breeze caressed my skin. I inhaled deeply but another bout of coughing rocked me. A quick look around revealed no other survivors nearby.

I didn't particularly want to meet any either. With my luck, it wouldn't be my girls but one of the other scientist freaks, some psycho guard, or a serial killer inmate.

Crouching by the pod's wreckage, I used the laser scalpel to cut two strips from the surgery blanket. I wrapped them around my feet and made a toga out of the remaining fabric. It barely covered my lady parts, but it beat streaking in the middle of bumfuck nowhere.

Where the hell am I?

To my right, far in the distance, the silhouette of a mountain loomed. The reddish tinge below the dark clouds above it, hinted of volcanic activity. I'd had my fill of fire to last me a lifetime. To my left, a field of high grass ran in a straight line as far as the eye could see. I suspected it hid a body of water. Up ahead, a woodsy area held the promise of food or game to catch. Behind me, a trail of the interstellar prison's wreckage covered a barren flat land.

With a determined gait, I headed for the woods.

Chapter 2

LYDIA

My muscles trembled as I entered the shade of the forest. Hunger twisted my insides, leaving me weak and light-headed. I didn't know where we had crashed, but it sure as hell wasn't Kansas. The pale outline of the two moons hanging in the clear blue sky tipped me off that we were on some uncharted planet. Now traipsing through the forest, evidence abounded, even though the flora looked similar to that from Earth, with subtle variations in colors, sizes and textures.

Despite the flimsy protection covering my feet, I painlessly walked over soft green grass and spongy brown soil. The tree leaves leaned closer to a bluish tint than Earth's traditional green. Flowers in both common and exotic shapes boasted brighter-than-usual colors, some bordering neon or appearing to glow. The scent of wet vegetation and complex flowery fragrances swirled around me. I took a few deep breaths to chase away the lingering stench of the smoke.

Let's just hope the air isn't filled with some messed up toxin.

The fauna, however, was a completely different beast—literally. The flowy petals of a beautiful red flower took off in flight when I came near it, too fast for me to say if it was a bird or a giant insect. Twenty minutes later, I leaned on a tree only to have a section of the bark hiss at me. The furry chameleon-like critter it belonged to crawled up the tree while glaring at me with indignation.

Sorry?

How was I supposed to know when everything made a point of it to use some form of camouflage? I didn't notice the smaller critters until I all but stepped on them. I couldn't tell if it was a trick to hide from predators or to lure unsuspecting prey; probably a mix of both. Although I could hear birds, I'd yet to see one aside from that flying-flower-thing. The few mammals I managed to spot were on the tiny side and scurried about like they feared they wouldn't get all of their tasks done before some curfew.

A blood-chilling screech in the distance made me change direction. I had no intention whatsoever of making the acquaintance of anything that sounded like that. The birds' chirping and bugs' buzzing going silent for a few seconds, too many seconds, further reinforced that notion.

My stomach rumbled as I came up to a small tree burdened with clusters of bright red berries. They reminded me of cranberries. My hand reached out for them before pausing. Were they cranberries or an alien version of the poisonous holly berries or cotoneaster? I chewed my bottom lip, reason telling me to back away while hunger pressed me to gorge on every morsel.

I counted at least four more similar trees with their branches sagging from the weight of the colorful fruits. If they were safe, why hadn't the local fauna eaten any? Under different circumstances, I would take the risk since my body could process pretty much any poison. That's what had gotten me unjustly incarcerated in the first place. But while my system fought the toxins, I'd be a sitting duck, vulnerable to anything that came at me.

Dropping my hand with regret, I stepped away and resumed my trek through the woods. Although I couldn't hear the river, I kept moving parallel to it, or so I hoped. While food remained my top priority, water stood as a close second. In retrospect, I should have confirmed a river indeed lay beyond those tall reeds. I'd do so as soon as my belly no longer clamored for food. Sobin had been starving me too long and if I had to make any use of my abilities, I'd become too weak to function.

A slurping sound drew my attention. It took me a moment to make out the small creature crouching by the gnarly roots of a tree. The animal stood no taller than a bunny. Slim, with a wide, flat head, I wouldn't have noticed it as its green fur blended almost perfectly with the grass and underbrush. Its red, long, lizard tongue gave it away when it darted out to snag a purplish growth on the tree roots.

Are they mushrooms?

My stomach growled and the creature's head snapped up. Its owl-like yellowish eyes connected with mine. It paused mid-chew, its body tense, no doubt ready to bolt. Although cute and seemingly cuddly, I didn't trust the little critter not to hide monster teeth behind that innocent face and have me for its main course. Raising my hands in surrender, I backed away slowly and it seemed to relax. Keeping its wary gaze on me, it resumed its meal.

Eyes darting in every direction, I looked for another patch of those mushrooms at the base of nearby trees. Finding one within seconds, I threw myself at them with wild abandon and stuffed my face, heedless of their bitter taste. After the seventh or eighth mushroom, I forced myself to slow down. Making myself sick now wouldn't be wise in this unknown, and possibly hostile, environment.

My hand reached for another flat mushroom when the eerie silence struck me. I stopped chewing, my ears perking up. No more bird calls and no more insects buzz. Even the green bunny had abandoned its feast. The tree branches hung too high for me to reach, so there'd be no climbing to safety. I looked around, choosing a new direction to run. None seemed better than the next.

Head for the river.

A warbling call to my right was quickly echoed by four or five more behind. My blood curdled and I ran, arms pumping. Rocks, roots and dried branches stabbed the soles of my feet. Fear coiled in my belly as the calls of my assumed hunters resounded far too close for comfort.

Where the hell is that river?

Had I been heading the wrong way? Was I even now headed in the right direction? Fighting back the panic wanting to settle in, I kept running, my eyes peeled in search of anything I could use as a weapon. Lungs and legs burning from the effort, I entered a small clearing.

I pitched forward, almost falling on my face as my feet sank into muddy ground. Momentum carried me four or five more steps before I could stop, calf-deep in some kind of quicksand. Heart pounding, I tried to backtrack when movement in the trees caught my attention. My head snapped up and my eyes latched onto my pursuer. Shifting branches in nearby trees revealed four more smaller creatures surrounding me.

The first one, their mother I presumed, measured at least two meters long. Almost the same color as the tree branches, she possessed ten multi-jointed, spear-like limbs, spread along her body. On her chest, a pair of arms ended in two long-clawed digits. Half her limbs wrapped over her back to hold onto the branch above while her remaining limbs dangled at the ready, to capture, impale or propel her forward as she raced to catch her prey.

To catch me.

Violet frills rose around her head as she opened her toothy jaw to emit another warbling call. Her babies answered.

My heart hammered against my ribs as the creatures closed in. I fisted my laser scalpel, knowing it wouldn't be much help. The quicksand wasn't deep but would slow me too much to outrun them. Flaring up wouldn't save me from getting mortally stabbed by their spears.

But hardening the mud would let me run.

Without giving it further thought, I dropped my temperature as low I as I could. Within seconds, the mud thickened around me and a small film of frost covered my skin. My skin had never done that before but I didn't have time to marvel at the phenomenon. What little of the latest serum I'd received seemed to have enhanced me further.

The hunters screeched, their tiny heads turning this way and that, as if looking for something. The mother dropped from the branch, landing on her spindly limbs like a centipede. She looked around the small clearing, her eyes gliding over me, as if I didn't exist.

She can't see me…

Her young dropped from their trees as well, circling the edge of the quicksand pond, their reptilian eyes searching.

Infrared! They're blind without body heat!

My heart soared and I forced myself to control my labored breathing. Their small, pointy ears drooped alongside their heads. Who knew how sensitive they were. Grateful for the noise of their angry warbling as they sought their prey, I tiptoed out of the quicksand, adjusting my temperature to avoid causing a cold draft. Giving them as wide a berth as possible, I snuck past them and made a bee line for the tall grass finally visible ahead. I peeked over my shoulder to make sure they hadn't resumed pursuit. The mother, her front legs sinking into the quicksand, swiped at empty air, searching for me.

Drawing in a shuddering breath, I hastened to the river, hoping to reach it before I became too weak to maintain my cool temperature. Clearing the tree line at last, I knotted the scalpel into the folds of my toga then ran into the tall grass. Only once surrounded by their sharp blades scratching my arms did I pause to wonder if something worse than the giant lizard-monkey-centipede things hid in the reeds.

What about the water? Are there piranhas in there?

The trickling song of the river beckoned me. Its crystalline water revealed nothing threatening. I waded in until it covered my shoulders. Welcoming its cold embrace, I released my frost and returned my temperature to normal. The weak current led away from the crash site of the *Concord*. Arms spread, legs stretched, I let it carry me. My stomach felt queasy, no doubt from all the stress. While trying to relax, I kept a careful eye out for anything rising from the depths to eat me or any menace from the shore.

The pleasant coolness of the water and its gentle sway as it flowed lulled me, soothing my weariness. Small, silver fishes with a rainbow-shimmer jumped around, reminding me of flying fish back on Earth. I smiled at the colorful display.

A sharp cramp in my stomach pulled me out of my daze. For a while, I'd been getting that roiling sensation one often gets in an elevator but blamed it on motion sickness from the waves. Another vicious contraction forced me to straighten and tread water. The strength of the current surprised me. I hadn't noticed when it had picked up so much.

As I turned toward the shore, excruciating pain doubled me over. I retched, my face dipping into the river.

The mushrooms...

The cold water bit my burning skin even as a wave of dizziness weighed me down. I fought the current, slowly moving toward my goal. Another round of dry heaves eroded what little progress I had made, dragging me further down the river and away from the bank. Heart thumping, my arms seemed to move in slow motion while I fought my way back to the surface. They felt heavy and weak. Cramps shot through my stomach, tortured by an unfulfilled need to hurl. Water rushed into my nose and throat, burning and choking my airways as my body sank. Kicking my feet, I emerged and gasped for air.

The heightened speed of the river's flow and the thundering sound in the distance only increased my panic. Given enough time, my enhanced body could process poison but not drowning or crashing on the rocks at the bottom of a waterfall. Unable to battle the current's inexorable pull, I focused on keeping my head above water through the spasms seizing my muscles.

When the frothing edge of the waterfall loomed before me, I closed my eyes and addressed a silent prayer to anyone listening.

And then I was weightless, wrapped in a curtain of water, cold air whipping around me.

―――✠\\⌓―――

THE EARTH SHAKING BENEATH me roused me to consciousness. A little dazed and confused, it took me a moment to remember what had been going on before I blacked out.

I cracked my eyes open and beheld nothing but icy snow. Water licked my feet and calves while my upper body rested face down on, or rather partially in, a bank of frozen snow. Aside from hunger—my now constant companion—and weariness, I couldn't feel any injury.

Pushing myself up, a layer of ice and snow on my back broke, crumbling down around me. My toga felt like cardboard, frozen almost solid around me. I'd been resting in a melted outline of my body, having no doubt flared up to burn the poison from the mushrooms. The amount of snow and thickness of the ice that covered me implied I'd likely been unconscious for a couple of days after washing up on the bank.

The ground continued to shake. Each tremor lasted two seconds, followed by a heavy thump in the distance. The regularity of the interval between each quake made me think of the steps of a giant out for a stroll.

Don't tell me they've got dinosaurs too!

Under the twin moons illuminating the night, a tall cliff, maybe a hundred meters high, framed the waterfall. From where I stood, I couldn't tell if the cliff was made of white stones or covered in snow. Although the scene was picturesque, I only cared that the thundering steps of whatever thing caused the ground to tremble came from somewhere beyond that cliff, far away from me.

I turned in the opposite direction and my breath caught in my throat. In the distance, large white structures, clustered together like a city, stood beneath a mesmerizing shimmer like the Northern Lights. The man-made—well, constructed city—sat near the river and appeared to float on a sea of ice. As far as the eye could see, the land lay flat with occasional snowbanks.

There would be no hiding my approach from anyone that might be watching…

Unfrozen

I crouched and cupped my hands in the water before lifting them to my mouth. The icy cold water—just the way I liked it—tasted clean and fresh. I drank until it sloshed in my stomach, hoping it would dampen my gnawing hunger. Rising to my feet, I adjusted my torn toga that had somehow survived the ride, including the laser scalpel still knotted in the folds. I inhaled the cool, crisp air and marched towards the city. Nothing could be heard in the empty, frozen land besides the crunching of my bare feet breaking through the thin layer of ice covering the snow. Well, nothing aside from the chattering of the running river and the distant thumping.

I didn't mind the cold. In fact, I welcomed it. Hopefully, the citizens would welcome me. Living in this arctic climate with my hot flashes would provide me with some much appreciated relief.

I haven't had one in a while.

That thought gave me pause. By the time I'd passed out on the bank, I'd been traipsing around the forest and floating down that river for at least three hours. Not once since awakening from the crash had I experienced a hot flash when I normally got multiple ones every hour. Could the last injection have fixed me?

What a relief that would be!

I also couldn't see any bruises or injuries on my body from the crash or from the nicks and cuts sustained while fleeing in the forest. It had to be another blessing from Quinn's serum.

While hoping my hot flashes were a thing of the past, a greater relief would be food, a shower, and rest. I was running on fumes. Each step made my legs shake with fatigue and my heart sink in despair. After trudging through the snow for what felt like an hour, I climbed the stairs to the entrance of a city that showed no sign of life.

The statue of a woman greeted me. At least five meters high, she held her arms outstretched like a mother beckoning her child. The thick layers of old snow covering her and the buildings beyond belied the warmth of her welcome. The streets had not been cleared in months, if not years. Even the wind didn't bother howling between the white-walled alleys of the ghost town.

Who would have abandoned such a wonder and why?

The city reminded me of a Mayan village, with a tall pyramid erected at the edge of a massive plaza. Rectangular buildings of varying height and width, with flat rooftops, surrounded the city square. A few towers and decorative pillars stood proudly, bearing giant cameos of the statue I'd seen at the entrance. Made of the same white stones, each building boasted intricate tribal patterns carved into their facades. The ice covering the ornate walls and the icicles dangling from the rooftops reflected the Northern Lights in a hypnotic dance.

Feasting my eyes wouldn't fill my belly, though. I'd taken a couple of hesitant steps forward when a glowing light to my left drew my attention. I recoiled, my heart all but leaping out of my chest when my gaze landed on two men, standing still in some kind of alcove.

Not men... statues.

My hand rested over my chest, trying to contain my erratic pulse. Leaning forward, I squinted, making sure my eyes weren't playing tricks on me. I moved closer, noting the same type of complex carvings on the front surface of the alcoves. A glowing, jelly-like substance lit the patterns from within in a beautiful, soft halo of reds, yellows and blues.

Unfrozen

The statues, erected on each side of a staircase going down, stood over two meters tall. Their features, not quite human, bore many similarities. Despite their closed eyelids, their eyes appeared bigger, with a sharp brow ridge and almost crystalline eyebrows. A flat, narrow nose bridge flared at the base with two tiny holes for nostrils in a bee-sting bump of a nose tip. The wide mouth had a thin bottom lip and a near non-existent upper lip deprived of a cupid's bow.

At first, I believed them both to be bald, but something akin to a single thick braid protruded at the back of their head, like the ancient pharaohs. I ran my fingers along the ear, shaped like the fanned fins of a fish with a hole at the base. The hard, yet somewhat soft texture startled me. I recoiled, my eyes flicking back up to his still closed eyes. He neither breathed nor moved. My gaze lowered to his chest where a big hole gaped at me. Damage hadn't caused this. It looked engineered; an insert slot for something like a large battery.

Are they cyborgs?

That would explain the almost fleshy feel of their ice blue skin, and maybe even their not quite human appearance. On Earth, since the early talks of androids, the ethics panels all agreed that any artificial intelligence shouldn't be given the perfect likeness of a human to avoid potential confusion.

These *statues* stood naked. Their muscular, very human-like bodies were on full display but for some kind of a loincloth. My face heated as I chased the thought of lifting it to look underneath. I wanted to believe it was out of respect of his—its?—modesty. Even as I stomped down the urge, curiosity would have me wondering for a while yet.

Then it struck me.

Unlike in the rest of the city, snow didn't cover these statues or the path leading downstairs.

Someone is maintaining them. Has the population moved below?

With one last wary glance at the statue-cyborg things, I descended the stairs. On the right a huge archway, lit with the same fancy patterns, led into an underground city.

"Wow…" I whispered.

Ice palace were the first words that came to mind. Although, it wasn't ice at all. Well… only partially. The archway opened on a greeting hall the size of a basketball field. The ornate white stone walls, at least four meters high, smoothly arched into a ceiling boasting complex carvings reminiscent of exquisite Moroccan plasterwork. The same glowing texture between the creases, this time of various colors, lit the patterns with a soft glow. The thin sheet of ice covering the arabesques made the whole thing glitter like iridescent diamonds.

In each corner of the room, a pedestal held a large, polished glow-stone which bathed the room in a soft rainbow of red, yellow and blue light. A larger version with multiple stones sat in the center of the hall. But it was the two dozen or so alcoves along the walls that made my heart flutter.

Each one contained another of those humanoids. The majority of them had their eyes open, although they stared ahead, unseeing. Under the soft light in the room, the skin of the handful with their eyes closed appeared duller than that of the others.

Are they disabled?

I approached one of them with careful steps, my bare feet silent on the granite-like floor, ready to bolt at the first sign of danger. Stopping in front of him, I waved my hand before his vacant eyes.

"Hey! Are you there? Are you awake?"

As expected, no response. I snapped my fingers next to his ear, but still no response. My shoulders sagged, the tension I hadn't realize knotted them draining. Unable to resist, I touched his muscular chest, the cold, hard skin yielding more than the previous guy's. My gaze flicked back up to his to see if his expression had changed but still nothing. Drawn to the opening in his chest, my fingers traced the contour.

Something definitely goes there.

Maybe if I found it and reactivated one, he could help me out. Then again, maybe he'd chop me to pieces and serve me as appetizers.

A tingling sensation at the back of my head made me turn around. Looking at the other ice men lining the walls, they all appeared as inert as before, yet the uncanny sense of being observed didn't abate. Although they stared ahead, it felt as if their eyes were following me in that creepy way portraits sometimes did. Anyway, it was time for me to move further into the *palace* to search for whoever was doing the shoveling outside.

The thick silence unnerved me as I exited the hall into a wide corridor. Beyond, I crossed a large room with countless tables and long benches that could serve as a cafeteria, conference room or workshop. Its purpose? No clue. But the absence of anything remotely resembling a stove or cooking device convinced me this was no kitchen.

A wave of dizziness reminded me that my body needed refueling asap. I leaned against the wall for a few seconds until the lightheadedness subsided. Pushing on, the next room contained nothing but shelves with various tools made of stone and wood. I didn't waste time studying them. There'd be plenty of time for that later... I hoped. A number of corridors shot off from the main hallway, but I chose not to explore them for now. I didn't want to get lost. Also, if I needed to make a run for it, racing down the main corridor back to the entrance felt like a good plan.

None of the rooms had doors. As I reached the next opening, I squealed with excitement. Before me lay a giant football-field sized underground garden or greenhouse type of thing. Tall grass resembling wheat and other types of vegetables had died and dried in the field. I wouldn't get much out of that. However, some type of bushy vine crept up the wall, clusters of plump red berries similar to those I had snubbed in the forest called out to me. I rushed toward them, my excitement turning to panic. Even knowing they hung out of reach, I jumped a few times, arm stretched, in an effort to grab some.

Groaning in frustration, I scanned the greenhouse for something that would allow me to get to them. Saliva flooded my mouth as another rumble rose from my painfully empty belly. My eyes latched onto some kind of basin with a series of yellowish spheres the size of a cantaloupe. I remembered seeing them on trees in the forest, the lowest branch too high for me to climb.

Forgetting the berries, I dashed for the basin and picked up the fruit, its bumpy surface rough against my skin. Although it weighed about the same as a watermelon, its shell was harder than a coconut. Try as I might, I couldn't get the damn thing open. To make matters worse, my stomach kept rumbling and cramping as if it knew food was within its grasp but was being denied.

I raised the coconut-melon above my head, ready to smash it against the wall in the hope of cracking it open when I remembered my scalpel. Putting the fruit back in the basin, I fumbled through the folds of my toga, taking more time than necessary in my impatience. I all but ripped it out, swallowing more saliva. The scalpel cut through it like butter and the sweet smell of caramelized sugar tickled my nose. The fruit parted, its white flesh filling the air with a tantalizing scent.

With two fingers, I dug in, bringing some of the gooey texture to my lips. I poked my tongue at it. My eyes widened at the exquisite taste. I shoved my fingers into my mouth.

Holy shit!

It tasted like a mix of mango and papaya with a dab of honey. I gulped down the first half of the fruit, scooping out the mushy goodness by the handful and cramming it into my mouth. I don't think I chewed once. I had started on the second half with the same enthusiasm when the feeling of being observed stopped me.

My head jerked up as I surveyed the room. Again, there was no one in sight. I had been so intent on stuffing my face I'd forgotten this could be a hostile environment. Someone could have snuck in without my notice. For all I knew, they could be hiding in the dead crop right now, ready to lunge at me. My back tensed and my pulse picked up a tad.

"Is anyone there?"

No answer.

I didn't really expect one. Hugging the second half of the alien melon to my chest, I resumed eating. This time, I slowed down a bit and kept my eyes on the room for any sign of trouble. Still hungry, I cut a second one. If some predator lurked in the crop, the sight of my scalpel might make him think twice.

By the time I finished, my brain finally caught up with my stomach being full... overly so. I stacked the empty shells in a neat pile by the basin and clambered to my feet. Feeling a little groggy as one often does after overindulging, I licked my sticky fingers and examined the room some more. I needed to find some water, not only to clean myself up but also to wash down some of the sweetness lingering in my mouth. Sugar always made me thirsty.

A sprinkler system ran through the crops and along the wall, but I couldn't see the water source. In the ceiling, a large angled opening allowed the sun to shine in, its rays deflected towards the crop with a strategically laid out mirror system.

Turning around, I headed out of the greenhouse. I found neither a bathroom nor a kitchen, but a hot spring. With a squeak of delight, I ran up to the stony edge and dipped my toes in the water.

Perfect!

Compared to the brightly lit and ornate rooms from before, this one was empty and covered in shadows. Some light did trickle in from tiny openings in the ceiling and from the hallway. Along the walls, some clusters of lights bathed the room in a soft glow. I first thought they were bioluminescent mushrooms but then one of them moved.

Fireflies.

Or something along those lines.

It struck me that the hot spring didn't reek of sulfur as was often the case. In fact, the room didn't have any particular smell, other than my own sweaty self.

Ugh.

The feeling of being observed having subsided again, I removed my toga and slipped into the warm water, placing the scalpel on the roughly cut edge, within easy reach. The water rose to my chest. A couple of steps in sufficed for it to lap at my chin. I moaned as the pleasant heat seeped into my muscles, releasing the tension accumulated over the past months of my incarceration.

For a fleeting moment, I wondered if anyone else had made it out. I couldn't imagine that no one else survived the crash. Being a social person, I didn't really want to be alone, but the thought of any of them finding this place scared me.

Although this underground city appeared abandoned, I believed whoever had cleaned the steps lurked around, maybe as afraid of me as I was of them.

What if they have already encountered some of the inmates or the guards? What if things have gone wrong and made them suspicious of me?

I'd been out cold for at least a day but more likely two while my body processed that poison. If I had found this place, others could too.

My eyelids drooped. Between today's stress, the soothing warmth of the hot spring and the bliss of a full belly, my body now demanded rest. Pulling my ragged 'toga' into the water, I washed it before climbing out of the spring. I wrung the water out of the fabric, wrapped it around my still wet body, and then I flared up a bit. A slight vapor rose in the cool air from my skin and the toga.

I trudged back to the hallway and looked for a place to sleep. The tingling sense of being watched returned. Either my stalker had the same camouflage skills every other creature on this planet seemed to possess, or I'd become completely paranoid. Whatever the case, I couldn't do much about it, so I tried not to let it bother me. They'd come out when they were ready.

The corridor ended in a steep cliff. I could see another level below but no way to get there. After much hesitation, I backtracked to one of the offshoot corridors I had snubbed earlier. It wound on a short distance before branching off. I followed the right hall which opened up a few meters later on a bedroom. It looked as if it came straight out of those ice hotels I'd visited back on Earth.

Like all the previous rooms, they kept the furnishing to a minimum but went all out on the lattice work on the walls. I approached the massive bed made of a single slab of ice and ran my fingers over the thick white fur covering it. In the corners, pedestals with glow stones—the only other items in the room—provided the ambient lighting.

Although tempted to lie down, I decided to do a quick check of the other rooms in case there was anyone else around or asleep. By the ninth empty bedroom, having gotten turned around a few times, I gave up. Casting all prudence aside, I crawled onto the bed. Despite the hardness of the ice slab, the fur felt plush and comfortable. No sooner did my head rest on my forearm than darkness swallowed me.

Chapter 3

KAI

The strange female intrigued me. When I first saw her approach the city, I thought the Creators had returned. Until she drew closer. Her coverings looked nothing like the colorful fabrics worn by our masters. The smooth lines of her face, dark skin and the long, curly hair on her head, corrected me of that mistake. The Creators' features, sharp and angular, were easy to carve into stone, ice or snow. Hers would require far more finesse.

A worthy challenge.

Curled up on the orzarix pelt, she looked small and fragile in her sleep. Well, she *was* small, at least three heads shorter than a Creator. Her efforts to catch the gurahn berries had been pointless. It had made me wonder at her intelligence until she used that glowing knife to cut the riverfruit. A primitive creature couldn't have made the connection to use a tool this way, and not with such dexterity.

The way she had devoured them, she must not have eaten for days. I hadn't eaten in centuries, didn't need to, not since the change. Her blissful expression as she ate and the purring rising from her throat made me believe she liked the taste. The Strangers had liked them too but refused to eat them raw. We had many preparations for riverfruit. As our Creator Tarakheen used to say, one should strive to elevate and refine all that one makes.

The female stirred, mumbling incoherent words in that foreign language of hers. She'd done that a few times during her sleep. I wondered if it was a common trait of her species. Many hours had lapsed since the beginning of her rest cycle.

How much time does she require to rejuvenate?

The sun had risen at least three hours ago. The Strangers and their leader, Tarakheen, would have already been up and about, demanding we cater to their needs.

Will she expect me to cater to hers?

Where did she come from? Why was she here? Was she lost or looking for something? I'd been observing her as she traipsed about our city, ready to intervene if she threatened my people. I almost attacked her when she touched my brothers and poked at their heartstone encasing. But the gentle way she ran her fingers over them, with a look I could only interpret as wonder, stayed my hand.

I looked at the food I had set on a table next to the bed. The Strangers liked to eat first thing in the morning. It lifted their spirit and lightened their mood. Happy Strangers meant less strenuous days for the valos. However, the female wasn't a Stranger. I didn't think she could use compulsion on us like they had.

Maybe she's their child?

The thought troubled me. I eyed the female again. She definitely wasn't a valo like me or any other types of valo built by the Creators in the other cities. Her skin coloring didn't match Tarakheen's people, but that didn't mean there weren't brown-skinned Creators. Both her lips were plump and full, with an interesting dip in the middle of the upper one. The Strangers had no lips, a single slit served as their mouth opening. My index finger ran over my upper lip. It was thin, almost non-existent, but my bottom lip was somewhat similar to hers.

No. The female was alien to anything I knew. The arc of her hairy eyebrows, the gentle slope of her nose bridge, the round ears, the swelling mounds on her chest, the flaring of her hips... Curves defined her. Truly a worthy challenge. I couldn't decide what material I would carve her likeness in. Stone would last longer but might prove tricky.

As I stood waiting for the female to awaken, I reflected on an appropriate pose for the statue. I wanted to give her face the same expression she'd had when her naked body first entered the burning waters. It had been centuries since I had witnessed anyone express such levels of bliss. Without my heartstone, I no longer felt those kinds of emotions... I barely felt at all.

She enjoys heat.

Since the change, my people no longer entered those waters. The Creator turned our bodies into temples of ice and frost. We couldn't withstand much heat anymore, although our genetic memory craved certain levels of warmth. The hot pond didn't burn us on contact. However, exposure for more than a few seconds caused extreme discomfort, and blisters would form if we remained in the water beyond a few minutes. She stayed in for a long time, unharmed.

Like the Creator...

How much of it could she tolerate? Could she handle the inferno of the magma? My fingers probed the hollow inset in my chest. That odd sensation tugged at me again, like every other time I thought of my missing heartstone. As I didn't feel desire of any type anymore, I could only attribute it to instinct, this *need* to have it restored. What would it be like to feel again?

Another twenty minutes went by with the female still sleeping. Wanting to be here when she woke up kept me from going upstairs to clear the snow and ice off my dead brothers standing vigil outside. The guards had been among the first to lose the will to live and return to Sonhadra. Over the past decades, a few more had followed, their eyes closing forever.

Most of the recent deaths belonged to the Miner cast. After the departure of the Strangers, they continued to strip the mines, stockpiling the gems and metals Tarakheen had demanded until nothing remained. The Strangers never returned for them, or us. With no more resources to dig up and no new task, they lost their purpose. After lingering for a few centuries, one by one, they went into hibernation, from which many would not rise again. The Builders followed, then the Hunters and Gatherers, then finally, my class, the Crafters.

From time to time, one of my brothers would awaken and keep me company for a few hours, days, weeks, and on extremely rare occasions, for months before they returned to their alcove. That also gave me that strange little tug every time they left or one of my brothers died.

Before they went back, a few of them asked me why I didn't hibernate, too. Unlike the others, I still had a purpose. As an artist, there was always more to do, more to *elevate and refine*.

My head perked up when the female stirred again. Her eyelids fluttered and she rolled onto her back. She took a deep breath and then, muscles tensing, she stretched her limbs as far as they could extend, lifting them slightly above the bed. Her features strained and the long, drawn out moan that escaped her lips sounded almost painful. For a moment, I wondered if she was having some kind of a seizure. Then her arms and legs flopped back down onto the fur. Her features relaxed and her muscles loosened. She looked boneless as she heaved a sigh.

Unfrozen

What a strange creature.

She opened her eyes, blinked at the ceiling, and started to sit. At last, her gaze landed on me. She froze, lips parting and eyes widening. The piercing sound of her scream hurt my ears. I flinched while she scrambled backwards until her back hit the bedhead. Eyes glued to my face, her hands fumbled blindly with the folds of her coverings until she pulled out the glow knife from last night. To my surprise, she didn't threaten me with it but held it to her chest like a shield. I didn't doubt for a minute she would brandish it if I moved closer.

I stood still, at the foot of the bed, giving her some time to calm down. Her gaze roamed over me before settling back up on my face.

I should have made a chair.

In comparison to her, I was quite tall—at least two heads above her. Sitting on the bed, she craned her neck to look at me as I towered over her. Sitting would have also made me appear less threatening. With slow, measured steps, I moved to the left side of the bed. Her body jerked and she moved back to the edge of the bed on the opposite side. Keeping close to the wall, I stopped near the table laden with food.

She glanced down at it, noticing it for the first time. Her throat worked and a pink tongue peeked out between her lips to moisten them. Frown lines marred her forehead as her eyes flicked between me and the table which hadn't been there last night.

Observing her reaction, I called upon the frost—a gift from the Creator—to solidify the water in the air. She made a shocked sound as a block of ice formed behind me. Despite the burning urge to do so, I didn't refine it, or make it pretty. It was a temporary accommodation for the purpose of putting her at ease.

Within seconds, I completed the task and sat down. Mouth wide open, her ice-blue eyes, striking against her dark skin, stared in turn at my seat then at me.

"*Oleeshet! Dat wazkool!*" she said.

I blinked. She was making those strange sounds again that held no meaning. However, the look on her face and the tone of her voice seemed to express appreciation. Although wary, she no longer trembled, the glow-knife still clutched against her chest.

"I do not know your words," I said.

She frowned and cast a brief glance at my mouth.

"*Wawaz dat?*" she asked.

It was my turn to frown. Communicating would prove challenging with her strange language.

"What is your name? What are you?"

Her frown deepened and she tapped two fingers at the back of her ear.

"What? *Wyzdat teeng* not *werkin?*"

A couple of her words had made sense this time. Wherever she came from, they didn't speak the language of the Strangers or that of the Northern Valos.

She huffed, a frustrated expression on her face, then gave me an assessing look.

"*My naymz Leedya.*" She tapped the hand fisting the glow-knife against her chest twice. "*Lee-dya,*" she repeated, then pointed the weapon at me. "*Yoo?*"

Unfrozen

I frowned, my eyes locking on her glow-knife. There was no aggression in her stance or tone, but that didn't lessen the potential threat.

"*Oshet! Sawree! Sawree!*"

She shoved the hand holding the weapon behind her back and raised her other palm in an appeasing gesture. Fear strained her features. There was no need for it. She had lowered her weapon. All was well.

I tilted my head to the side. "Do not fear. I am not angered."

She grimaced, no doubt failing to grasp my words. Keeping the weapon hidden, she tapped her chest twice again.

"*Leedya. Lee-dya,*" she repeated then pointed her index finger at me. "You?"

Three words. We were getting somewhere. I couldn't say if Leedya was her name or her species but I assumed the former.

"Leedya," I said, pointing a finger at her.

She shook her head up and down with great energy, a large grin on her face.

"Yes! Lydia!"

"Lydia," I repeated, correcting my pronunciation... I hoped.

I placed my palm on my chest. "Qaezul'tek Var E'lek."

Her smile stiffened then faded, a stunned expression settling on her face.

"*Sae* what?"

"Qaezul'tek Var E'lek," I repeated.

She blinked, looking distraught. Did she not understand my meaning? I wondered once again at her intelligence.

"Lydia," I said, pointing at her, then at myself, "Qaezul'tek Var E'lek."

She shook her head up and down again, but this time with less enthusiasm. I suspected it was one way her people expressed agreement.

"Ryt." She cleared her throat. *"Kyzuk... Kyzeluk..."*

Oh! Too complex for her.

I'd never considered that. The Valos of E'lek all possessed long names since they carried a lot of information about the individual. Qaezul'tek Var E'lek was the formal way to introduce myself. My actual given name was Qae of the Zul bloodline, third male of that name in my bloodline—pronounced tek in the old tongue—and Var, meaning firstborn child. Since many of my people used to live a nomadic life, we specified the name of our tribe; in my case, the heart of the Northern Valos tribes, the city of E'lek.

My brothers usually called me Qaezul or Qae. I decided to put an end to her misery.

I pointed at her. "Lydia," then at myself, "Qae."

Tension left her shoulders and a look of gratitude settled on her features.

"Kai," she said.

Her pronunciation wasn't quite accurate. She made is sound like die or rye when it should be more like kwy, but it was close enough. Somehow, I suspected I didn't say her name quite right either. I gestured to the food. She glanced at it and licked her lips.

"*Iz* that *furme?*" She pointed at the food then at herself.

"Yes."

Her eyes went straight to the riverfruit I had already cut in two halves, then to the fish steak sitting next to it. Hesitating between the two, she worried her bottom lip with blunt, white teeth. She scooted closer, casting wary glances at me, then carefully picked up the frozen square of red fish steak. The Strangers sometimes seared the spice-covered side on hot plates, but we had none in the lower-city, and I didn't know how to operate the ones in the upper-city.

Lydia looked at it, turning it from all sides before touching her tongue to the spices on the underside.

"*Mmhmm, taestee.*"

Although she was strange with all those weird sounds she made, I took this as a good sign. She opened her mouth and bit into it… or rather tried. Her blunt teeth completely failed to sink in at all.

"*Ow. Needz sum tahweeng.*"

She frowned at it and glanced in turn at the riverfruit, at me, then back at the fish. Lydia hesitated for a second then seemed to make a decision. Pushing her shoulders back, she lifted her chin and put down her glow-knife on the bed next to her. She then placed the fish in the center of her palm, spiced side up, and covered it with the other. Lydia kept her eyes on me as if fearing my reaction, then her palms—which looked almost white compared to the rest of her brown skin—turned pink, then a dark red. I tilted my head to the side, intrigued until I felt the small ball of heat emanating from her direction.

She IS attuned to fire!

Was it only her hands or could she control which part of her ignited like I did with frost?

She lifted one of her hands as her palms returned to their normal pale color. Although the fish had maintained its reddish hue, it had faded a little when its surface had started to cook. The spicy, seared fish aroma I had not smelled in centuries wafted towards me. It made me feel conflicted. It felt familiar and yet stirred the usual discomfort whenever we were reminded of the Creator.

She gave me an uncertain smile, looking somewhat worried. I didn't know what she needed from me, so I imitated her gesture of agreement and shook my head up and down. She giggled, the sound bright and bubbly bouncing through the room.

"That's *kyoot,*" she said, grinning, her worry fading.

Lydia lifted the fish with three fingers and raised the palm that had been holding it to her lips to slurp the thaw juice that had settled in it.

"*Mmhmmm.*"

That moan again, like when she ate the riverfruit last night. She licked her palm clean then bit into the fish. Her eyelids fluttered shut, as she tilted her head back, a blissful expression descending on her face.

"O gawd, sooo good!"

She repeated the thaw process a couple more times before she finished eating the fish. I would need to get more for her next time.

Why am I already thinking in terms of next times?

Unfrozen

She licked her palms clean then wiped her mouth with the back of her hand. Eyeing the riverfruit with greed, Lydia scooted closer to the table, picked up one half and shuffled back away from me. Like the previous night, she used her fingers to dig out the sweet flesh and eat.

"*Aye luv diss teeng.*"

"I do not know your words."

Blank look again. She didn't know mine either. Lydia made quick work of the first half and came closer to grab the second half. I reached for it first and she scrambled back, pressing the glow-knife against her chest again.

"Calm, Lydia," I said, as if speaking to a scared animal. "I will not harm you."

She didn't understand my meaning. Raising my hand to my face, I pointed my index finger at my eye then at the riverfruit.

"Lydia watch," I said.

Lydia followed the gesture and did that headshake.

"*Okay. Aye* watch."

Holding the hardened shell in the palm of my hand, I sent waves of cold seeping in. The shell frosted, its yellowish color taking on a darker, slightly greenish hue. I raised the index finger of my other hand, summoning the frost again to lengthen it into an icy spike. Eyes rounded, Lydia covered her mouth with her hand. She didn't seem frightened, so I continued. Dipping the spike into the sweet, white flesh of the fruit, I stirred it while sending more cool waves through it, until it formed some swirling, icy peaks. Releasing the ice spike at the tip of my finger, I used it to scoop some of the frozen riverfruit flesh. I willed it in the shape of an iwaki flower which grew around the city in the spring, with its spiky petals and long pistils in the center, using the ice spike as the stem.

"You are *reelee goodat diss.*"

Although I didn't understand half of her words, her tone and expression told me she appreciated my work. It encouraged me to continue. I shaped the other end of the ice spike as a spoon and stuck the edible flower in the largest swirl in the center of the riverfruit. I thought of decorating the edges of its hardened shell with intricate knots but forced myself to stick to a simple wavy trim. Once I started, I could go on forever.

Rather than putting it on the table, I leaned forward and extended the riverfruit to Lydia. If I couldn't get her to trust me, she wouldn't help me retrieve my heartstone.

The female stiffened, and after a slight hesitation, she scooted closer and carefully took it from my hand. She made as if to return to a safer distance from me then appeared to change her mind and stayed within arm's reach. With delicate fingers, she picked up the flower and brought it before her eyes, admiring it from every angle.

"*Sooo preetee!* You are *tahlinted.*"

Lydia licked one of the petals a couple of times before biting a piece off. Her pupils dilated, and she made that moaning sound again while sucking on the petal inside her mouth.

"*Taests eevin* better *lahk* that."

She ate the flower, smiling at me between each petal. A small layer of frost appeared over her hands, like the heat previously.

Is she also attuned to ice?

Once done with the flower, she gripped the stem with her frosted hand and scooped a mouthful of the riverfruit treat.

"*O waow! Lahk frootee ayescreem!*"

Whatever that meant, she liked it, and barely stopped to breathe while devouring the fruit. The Strangers never expressed this much appreciation. In fact, they didn't at all. Since perfection couldn't be achieved, only pursued, Tarakheen believed compliments and praise only encouraged mediocrity.

Lydia finished eating and stacked the empty shell casing of the riverfruit on top of the other.

"*Tank* you."

We stared at each other in a bit of an awkward silence. Not being able to communicate posed a major problem. I wanted to ask her to get my heartstone for me but didn't want her to think it was payment for the food.

She shifted, her gaze roaming around the room before settling back on my face.

"*Sooo* what *naow?*" she asked.

"I do not know your words."

Lydia grimaced in frustration, her shoulders slumping. Even though I couldn't feel, I understood her aggravation. Her face took on a pensive expression while she tapped her bottom lip with her index finger. A few moments later, her face brightened and she beamed at me. She lifted her left arm and a thin sheet of frost formed over it, turning it white.

"Kai watch," she said.

Emulating my earlier gesture, Lydia pointed a finger at her eyes then at her arm.

Intrigued, I tilted my head to the side and complied.

With the tip of her index finger, she drew three arches on her arm, and then made a primitive representation of a character inside each arch, like a child would.

Clever. I should have thought of it.

She pointed at her drawing, then towards the bedroom entrance.

She wonders about my brothers.

"Valos," I said.

"Valos?"

I shook my head up and down and indicated her arm. "Valos." I then placed my palm on my chest. "Qae is also valo."

"Hmm," she said, looking uncertain. Putting her palms together, she pressed the back of her hand against one cheek and leaned to the side, eyes closed. "Valos *sleep*," she said, before straightening, pointing at the drawing on her arm, then repeating the gesture.

Confused at first, understanding dawned on me as I recognized the pose from her rest cycle. I shook my head.

"Yes, the valos sleep."

She beamed. *"Naow wee goween sumware..."* Lydia pointed at me then repeated the process. "Kai not sleeping."

I understood that.

This time however, she had shaken her head from side to side when she said not. I memorized that as meaning no.

I shook my head up and down. "Yes," then from side to side as I said, "Qae not sleep."

She clapped her hands, grinning from ear to ear. I blinked at the odd behavior.

Strange female.

Lydia raised her hands before her, palms up and shrugged her shoulders in an exaggerated movement. *"Wy?"* she asked. *"Wy* valos sleep *but* Kai not sleep?"

I raised my hand and placed two fingers in the hollow casing in my chest.

"No heartstone."

"Batuhree ded?" She frowned and shook her head. *"*No, not *ded. Batuhree meessin?"*

I didn't know how to respond.

She gestured putting something inside her chest, then looked around the room like she was searching for something. Facing me back, she did that exaggerate shrug again. *"Ware?"*

This was the opening I needed. Explaining with words would be too complicated. Following her example, I indicated for her to look at the wall beside me. Summoning the frost, I drew five horizontal lines of ice, one stacked over the other. On the top line, near its center, I made an empty box.

"Lydia," I said, drawing a first dot inside the box. "Qae," I said putting a second dot next to hers.

I waved at the room then pointed to the square. She grinned and did the yes headshake. I wondered if she ever got a sore neck from doing that so often. Turning back to the wall, I traced three arches with the same stick figures she had done near the edge of the top line.

"Sleeping valos," she said.

"Yes. Very good, Lydia."

At the opposite end of the top line, I drew a diagonal line connecting it to the second line, then continued, in a zig-zag pattern, to connect the second to the third, the third to the fourth and the fourth to the last line. At the far end of the bottom line, I made a series of stacked circles.

"Heartstone," I said, pointing at the stack, then made of gesture of taking the stack and putting it in my chest.

To my surprise, she climbed off the bed and came near me to stand in front of the drawing. She pointed at me with her index finger, then raised it to my drawing. Without touching it, Lydia traced a path from the bedroom on the top floor, down the stairs connecting the floors, to the heartstone chamber on the bottom level. Once there, she pretended to grab the heartstone and put it in her chest.

I shook my head to indicate no. I couldn't just go fetch my heartstone.

"Why?" she asked.

I pointed at my eyes then at her, then waved my hand in a follow me gesture.

Lydia recoiled, then stilled, realizing at last how close to me she stood. She'd been too focused on the drawing to think of fearing me. A good sign that things were moving in the right direction. Not wanting to scare her, I took a couple of steps back, waving again for her to follow. Tension drained from her shoulders and an embarrassed, almost apologetic look crossed her features.

"*Okay,*" she said.

Unfrozen

'Okay' had to be another of her strange words for yes. Turning on my heels, I pretended not to see her fumbling with the folds of her coverings to secure the glow-knife there, and I led the way out of the room. As we emerged into the main hallways, I looked at her over my shoulder. She cast nervous glances around, especially towards the entrance hall where my brothers hibernated. If my sole presence unnerved her, it was reasonable to assume she feared being surrounded by more of the others.

"Calm, Lydia," I said in an appeasing tone. "The other valos sleep."

She gave me a sheepish look, her small fingers tugging at the hem of her coverings. Its ragged state and the rough, burnt edges of the dusty-blue fabric told me it had known better days. It didn't look like any dress I had seen before and made me wonder again where she had come from and what had led her here.

"Hangon," she exclaimed, as we walked in front of the hot pool.

She raced to the edge of the burning water. Dipping her hands in, she washed them, then splashed some of the hot liquid on her face. Like last night, her skin took on a slight reddish hue and the moisture covering her evaporated. Lydia sauntered back to my side, a happy smile gracing her features.

"Betuhr."

I crossed the short way to the edge of the cave. Lydia's steps faltered as we approached the cliff. Standing at a safe distance, she stretched her neck to look at the drop.

"No starez."

Lydia had looked for a way down last night for a while before giving up. I almost revealed myself then to tell her she was searching in vain. However, I wanted to get a better sense of her intentions before doing so and therefore remained hidden.

Before the Strangers' departure, their pets used to come here to steal some berries or roots from the field; a minor nuisance the Gatherers usually handled. The problems arose when they rampaged through the Crafter levels below, damaging the artisans' creations, and worse still, when they took to hiding their kills in the lower levels in places we couldn't reach and then forgot about them. The stench of decaying flesh would torture us for weeks. To avoid other such occurrences, we removed the stairways between the first and second floors. The Valos had faster, more convenient ways of climbing anyway.

I summoned the frost and a thick, icy platform took shape on the face of the cliff. I stepped on it and extended a hand to Lydia. Eyes bulging with fear, she shook her head to the negative in frenzy.

"*Aym skaird uf hyts.*"

She pointed at the drop down and mimicked a person falling down. Did she think I would push her off or was she merely afraid of heights? Hoping for the latter, I enlarged the platform and raised railings that would reach her chest.

Lydia eyed my work, chewing on her bottom lip. The panicked look on her face dimmed and she took a couple of hesitant steps forwards.

"Okay, that's *betuhr.*"

Unfrozen

She dragged her feet to the platform, gripped the edge of the railing and gave it a shake—or at least tried to—as if to tests its sturdiness.

Strange female.

I initiated the descent. Lydia squealed at the motion of the platform. One of her hands clasped around my wrist in a tight hold while the other gripped the railing. The warmth of her skin against mine seeped into my veins.

"Calm, Lydia. You are safe with me."

She tried to jump off as soon as we reached the second level, but I held her back until we reached the fourth one. By then, she no longer looked on the verge of passing out but didn't delay stepping off the platform the minute we reached the bottom. However, our final destination was one level lower, so we needed to use the stairs which still connected the levels two, three, four and five.

On our way to the stairs, her steps faltered then stopped as we passed in front of one of eight storage rooms on this level. This one contained countless stone and wooden containers filled to the brim with the colorful gems Tarakheen made the Miners harvest. The seven other rooms, twice the size of this one, contained the metal they mined. Eyes wide, mouth gaping, she appeared transfixed by the amount of gems.

"*Oleesheet!* That's *alotta rawks!* You *peepul mussbee lohded!*"

"I do not know your words."

She shook her head as if struggling to believe what her eyes were seeing.

"*Fuhget eet. Leedon.*"

She gestured with her head for us to keep moving and took two steps forward. A series of alcoves where my Miner brothers hibernated framed the stairs. A few more occupied the wall across from them. Lydia's gaze flicked frantically from one to the other. She had moved closer to me, subconsciously seeking my protection. Three of them—one more than yesterday—had their eyes closed. The others stared ahead with vacant eyes.

I waved a hand at them then mimicked the sleeping pose she had done earlier.

"No heartstone," I said, poking two fingers at the cavity in my chest.

She shook her head up and down yet still moved closer to me, our arms brushing against each other's as we came close to the pair of golems beside the stairs.

This was the longest staircase in the lower city. As we proceeded with our descent, the colorful, but gentle light of the glow stones soon gave way to the red-orange light of the lower level. The further down we got, the warmer it became.

"*Creepee*," Lydia whispered.

She cast an uncertain look towards me but followed nonetheless. We reached the bottom of the stairs and turned right onto the short corridor which extended into the path.

"*Oleesheet...* Is that *lava?*"

She said that word a lot. I was beginning to suspect it expressed awe, surprise, or shock.

Even from where I stood, the heat from the river of molten rocks tortured me. However, beyond the intense discomfort, my heartstone beckoned me. Many times before, I had tried to go after it, but the heat had forced me to turn back after only a few steps onto the path.

Lydia marched ahead, her face filled with wonder as she examined the room. Her skin flared with a reddish hue, like when she had thawed the fish, except her entire body this time.

"*Waow,*" she whispered when her gaze fell on the clusters of heartstones in the distance. "Are *doze* your *batuhreez?*" she asked, pointing at the clusters.

She turned to look at me and noticed at last that I hadn't followed her onto the path. Surprised, she frowned, then took in her surroundings and understanding dawned on her.

"*Ah,* yes*, too hawt fer* you.*"*

Backtracking her steps, she returned to me. I recoiled at the heat emanating from her flaring skin.

"*Oh sawree, sawree!*" she said, looking contrite as her skin returned to its normal brown hue. "*I go get fer* you.*"*

Lydia pointed at herself, then at the heartstone clusters, made a grabbing gesture then an offering motion towards me.

"Yes, please," I said, shaking my head up and down.

"Okay," she said. "*Weetch won?*"

Having realized that I didn't understand her question, she moved her hand around as if touching multiple objects grouped together, then picking one and putting it back down. Then she raised her hands before her, palms up, and shrugged her shoulders, a questioning look on her face.

She wants to know which one.

That was the problem. I didn't know which one and had no specific way of pointing it out to her. There were one-hundred-and-sixty heartstones split in five clusters. While I could feel it calling to me and would know it beyond any doubt if it lay before me, I had no distinctive way of identifying it for her.

I repeated her palms up shrug and shook my head side to side.

"I don't know."

Her shoulders slumped, and I wondered for a moment if she would say it was impossible and walk away. Pursing her lips, she glanced back at the clusters.

"*Guht* my *werk kuht out* for me *den*," she said in a discouraged tone. "*Bee ryt bahk.*"

Lydia turned on her heels and headed down the path towards the clusters. I felt the tug again but, this time, I could name the emotion lurking beneath: hope.

Chapter 4

LYDIA

Just when I thought my life couldn't get any freakier, it did with a capital F. Waking up to find Kai towering over me at the foot of my bed nearly gave me a heart attack. I mean, seriously, what kind of super tall, ice-colored guy, with a drool-worthy muscular body covered with nothing but a loincloth, and a flipping gaping hole in his chest would stare at you while you slept?

A cute and sweet valo named Kai.

I cast a glance at him over my shoulder. He still stood at the entrance of the magma room, looking mighty indisposed by the heat.

Yeah, Kai is cute.

Despite their alien appearance, his features were harmonious and his glowing, ice blue eyes hypnotized me. That he'd made a show of keeping a safe distance had helped alleviate my fears. That he'd fed me when I'd been so ravenous had earned him a lot of brownie points. But that crazy, delicious, beautifully decorated ice-cream-sorbet dessert he made for me? Now THAT won me over. A flower made of ice cream? I mean, you couldn't make something that good and that pretty and be a monster, right?

Kai didn't realize it but showing his ice manipulation ability had soothed an ache in my heart. After a lifetime of being different, Dr. Sobin had turned me into a full-on freak.

Humans would see me freeze or flare up and panic. Not Kai. He accepted it as normal and even seemed impressed. That had made me feel good. And now, I could do some good for him.

I gave Kai a smile then looked back at the room, although the word cave might be a more accurate description for it. Rough, darker stones than the white ones I'd seen everywhere before formed the walls of the cave, disappearing into the river of lava flowing at their base. Looking up at the ceiling, high enough to reach the top level of the lower-city, many large holes peeked on the outside making it resemble a giant colander.

I walked close to the wall down the six-meter-wide path which ran parallel to the lava river on its left. Up ahead, on a small island, a large stone altar glowed with about fifty ovoid-shaped luminous orbs: the valos batteries. The path circled around the island from the right. Against its outer wall, four more similar altars stood equally spaced out in an arc. Each contained about thirty orbs.

From a distance, it looked like a pulsating light had been trapped within a sphere of ice. But of course, the heat made that impossible. The altars weren't natural formations. Shaped like inverted step pyramids, their material was foreign to me. Despite their stony appearance, the texture beneath my fingers reminded me of some type of Kevlar. I suspected some kind of technology also helped preserve them.

The bumpy, darkened stone beneath my bare feet stabbed at my soles. I flared up to make the painful heat bearable. The path ran about twenty-five meters before turning right, following the cave wall, into a large circle around the island. At least ten meters of lava sprawled between the island and the edge of the path, preventing access onto it. Despite my flaring ability, I couldn't walk on lava. I'd get incinerated in seconds. If Kai's battery was one of those orbs, we were screwed.

I circled around the path, followed by the thick, bubbling sound of the lava and the slapping sound of my feet on the ground. The hot air made it hard to breathe, but fortunately, it didn't stink of sulfur as one would expect. Then again, neither had the hot spring. I vaguely recalled reading something about bacteria being responsible for that smell. It either didn't exist on this planet or in this area. Either way, that suited me just fine.

Coming up to the first altar, the cool breeze emanating from it confirmed my suspicions that some kind of mechanism helped preserve the orbs. Seeing them up close, they didn't quite qualify as orbs. They looked like stylized hearts made of a glass-like material and sat in a little recess like eggs in their tray. Inside the majority of the glass hearts, a blue light glowed with varying intensity. A handful had none. I suspected that this meant the valos they belonged to were no longer functional or had died.

The ones with their eyes closed...

A pang of sorrow shot through my chest. Although they still somewhat scared me, a life was a life, no matter how odd its appearance. I didn't know which one to choose, so I picked one at random. As soon as I held it, the light within flickered like a dying flame and it emitted the sizzling sound of water dropped on an overheated pan.

Shit! I'm burning it!

I immediately dropped it back into its slot. The light wavered like a stuttering heart before resuming its slow, pulsating glow.

How can I be so idiotic?

I'd just spent the past five minutes thinking about the cooling system then, like a moron, I went ahead and grabbed one with my skin all but ignited. Even my toga had darkened from my excessive body heat.

"This is gonna suck the big one," I muttered.

I lowered my temperature to match that of the hearts and touched it. No negative reaction. I would have called that great news except that now, the heat was kicking my butt. Leaving the hearts alone, I flared back up and moved toward the next altar. A cluster of orbs similar to those on the first altar welcomed me, except for one shining so bright it made me squint. My fingers itched to grab it but I held back, deciding to go check the other two altars before making a choice.

The remaining two altars held no surprises, each containing about thirty hearts of varying brightness. As I pondered which one to take, a number of disturbing thoughts made me second guess the wisdom of complying with Kai's request. I didn't know what Kai was, but I believed someone turned him and the other valos into what they were now. That hole in their chest looked far too engineered to be natural. My gut told me that the woman whose likeness plastered the upper-city had a heavy hand in it. Kai had shown me nothing but kindness so far, but he had also displayed as much emotion as a stone. He was frozen in every way. But what would putting his heart, battery or whatever the heck these orbs were, back inside him turn him into?

Looking at this setup, someone had gone through a great deal of trouble to make sure the valos would never get their hearts back without external help. A normal human wouldn't be able to retrieve them without special equipment and a cooling unit. There must have been a good reason to go to such extremes.

Unfrozen

What if giving them their hearts back turns them into monsters? What if they become insane cyborgs intent on assimilating or annihilating the world?

I shifted on my feet, not liking the direction of my thoughts one bit. One of the hearts on the altar before me dimmed but wasn't flickering like the one I had seen on the third altar.

Thankfully…

Despite my misgivings and fears, I had no doubt these guys would soon be dead if I didn't help reunite them with their hearts. Doing nothing meant committing genocide of these strange beings. I could never live with myself if that happened. It didn't eliminate the risk that they might turn into psychotic beasts, but I had to chance it.

Although I couldn't swear which heart belonged to Kai, the image of the brightest heart on the second altar danced in front of my eyes, luring me. Nevertheless, I would grab one heart from each altar and take it from there. It took me less than two seconds to lower my temperature enough that my skin frosted over. The heat hammered me, and my knees wobbled. The hot air, like a living entity, crushed me from all sides, stealing my breath and making my vision blurry. The frost on my skin melted and evaporated in puffs of steam. I lowered my temperature further to compensate. This would deplete me rapidly and made the heat worst.

I couldn't dally.

I reached a hand towards the altar, grabbed the dimmed heart, and cradled it in my arm against my chest to keep it cool. Retracing my steps, I dashed back to the third altar and grabbed the flickering heart. Placing it next to the first one, I ran to the second altar where I picked up the brightest heart.

Damn these things are heavy.

And big too. I had to wrap both my arms around them to hug them tight, but not too much. Despite their delicate appearance, they felt sturdy. Still, one could never be too cautious with someone else's heart, literally. At this point, I couldn't run and could barely even jog. The weight of the hearts held only a fraction of the blame. The heat burned my lungs, making my limbs heavy and my head drowsy. Reaching the first altar at last, I grabbed another bright heart before trudging along the path on my way back to the entrance.

My legs weighed a ton and my arms trembled from the strain. Descending into my lowest level of frost for such a sustained period while battling the heat, depleted my energy reserves at an exponential rate. The time I'd spent flaring while admiring the cave had already partially drained me. As I turned around the bend onto the twenty-five meter straight line to the entrance, the fear I wouldn't make it twisted my insides. If I collapsed now, I wouldn't die. My temperature would return to normal levels and I would pass out, only to come around once rested enough. It would be uncomfortable due to the heat but bearable. The hearts, though, wouldn't survive the extended contact with the overheated ground and air.

Up ahead, Kai showed the first signs of emotion. Eyes wide, features tense, he shifted restlessly as if fighting the urge to run forward and meet me halfway. He wasn't staring at me but at the hearts in my arms. The glow of the brightest one had steadily grown in intensity the closer I moved to the entrance... to Kai. I leaned against the rough stone wall for support as I dragged my feet forward. The distance eroded at a snail's pace. Kai spoke words I didn't understand; words of encouragement I assumed. Either way, the sound of his voice acted like a beacon, the lifeline I hung on to. With less than three meters to the entrance, Kai ran to me. His cold hands slipped under my knees and around my back. Picking me up, he ran us back to the entrance.

I collapsed against his broad, cool chest, and released my frost. It immediately stopped the loss of energy that had been pouring out of me like blood from a severed artery. With the hearts still cradled in my arms, I buried my face in the crook of Kai's shoulder. His gentle voice soothed me as he climbed the stairs back to the fourth level. I inhaled his unique scent, like the fresh, crisp air of an early spring morning. His cold skin wrapped around mine doused the fire that consumed me from within.

By the time we reached the top of the stairs, I had regained enough of my bearings to stand on my own... but barely. I didn't want him to put me down though, and it wasn't just because of the weakness that would continue to bog down my limbs until I had refueled. Being in his arms felt... safe. Since the beginning of the nightmare of my incarceration and the dreadful experiments performed on me, no one had showed the slightest inkling of protectiveness or concern for me.

Rather than climbing the rest of the stairs back to the top level, Kai carried me past a couple of rooms containing mountains of mined metal nuggets into what looked like another workshop with a handful of tables without chairs. He sat me on top of the nearest table and his inquisitive eyes looked into mine before lowering to the precious cargo in my arms.

I already knew which one belonged to him. Careful not to drop the other three, I lifted one hand, grabbed the brightest heart and offered it to him. Although subtle, an emotion crossed his alien features as he reached out with both hands to receive it. I placed it in his cupped palms and the heart's glow increased further in intensity. Kai stepped back, raised the heart before him, and then inserted it in the cavity in his chest. A blinding light stabbed my eyes, forcing me to look away.

Kai collapsed to his knees.

A drawn out, tortured scream tore from him. He clutched his chest, doubled-over on the floor. His body shook, and he threw his head back as another shout of agony rose from his throat. A cold shiver ran down my spine as I watched, helpless, his face contorting with excruciating pain. My arms tightened around the hearts still cradled against my chest and I debated whether to run for cover. I didn't understand what was happening, but Kai seemed to be morphing into something which I couldn't be sure wouldn't want to eat me or squish me.

The heart in his chest pulsated with a blinding ice-blue light, bathing him in a bright halo. All over his body, crystal-shaped ice shards of varying sizes protruded from his skin like armor. His body appeared to expand, gaining in mass and height. Kai's cry faded into a rumbling sound emanating from the depths of his chest. No longer trembling, he stopped clutching at his heart. His hands lowered to his sides and closed into fists resting on the cold, hard ground.

He's not a cyborg. He's some kind of ice elemental or golem.

With that realization also came the irrepressible urge to run, overriding the fear that had pinned me where I sat. I jumped off the table to my feet, and before I could take a single step, his head snapped up. Kai's glowing eyes bore into me, freezing me where I stood. My pulse raced at lightning speed and I forgot how to breathe.

"Calm, Lydia." His voice sounded doubled as if two different ones overlapped each other.

I understood that!

Unfrozen

Although I was freaked out by his current appearance, his eyes held no threat, only traces of the atrocious pain that had coursed through his body... and sadness. My survival instincts told me to haul ass as far away from him as possible, but my gut told me everything would be all right. This was the same Kai who had sculpted an ice cream flower for me. Plus, he hadn't lunged at me yet.

Kai slowly rose to his feet while the jagged ice armor covering his body receded back into him and his mass returned to normal. That went a long way into alleviating some of my fears. He hadn't gone insane and didn't seem to hitch with the urge to crush.

"Are you okay?" The trembling of my voice annoyed me.

"Yes, Lydia. I am. I remember."

I felt my eyes pop in my head as elation surged through me.

"I understand you! Do you understand me too?"

"I *berunate* you *um det.*"

"Ugh, never mind."

My shoulders drooped as disappointment struck me harder than it reasonably should. I was eager to communicate with him in a fluid manner. Still, in the few hours since we'd met, we'd made significant progress. I didn't quite understand why my universal translator didn't work properly. Well... Okay, I somewhat did. As far as I knew, Kai and I had made first contact between a human and an alien species. So, of course the translator wouldn't know his language and was working overtime to decipher it. We just needed to talk more to help it along. The headaches this process would give me would reach epic proportions.

Kai's hand indicated for me to retake my seat on the table. With great care, I laid down the three remaining hearts atop it, then hoisted myself next to them, grateful to get off my feet. My head still spun from my venture in the lava pit. Until I ate something to replenish my energy, I'd still feel a little woozy.

"Okay," I said, once settled.

Kai smiled.

Oh my God!

My hand flew to my chest in surprise. "You smiled!"

Kai tilted his head, a frown of confusion marring his forehead.

"You smiled," I repeated.

I pointed at my mouth, stretched in an exaggerated grin, then pointed at him.

Understanding dawned on him. Smiling again, he nodded in that clumsy but cute way he'd been doing from the moment he figured out that gesture meant yes. Kai tilted his head much too far in the back as if he wanted to look up at the sky, then brought his chin down almost to his chest. At this rate, he'd give himself a whiplash.

But damn, that smile is stunning! He's so freaking hot.

It lit up his entire face. Watching emotions play on his features was a marvel. It made him far less intimidating. Although he'd been nothing but kind to me, the cold, emotionless being he'd been before had creeped me out a little bit.

Kai placed a hand over his heart. It no longer blinded me but glowed with a slow pulse.

"*Merun* heartstone *fati* me *resnete* emotions," he said.

So, it's not hearts but heartstones.

But it didn't only make him feel emotions, it also seemed to have kicked his translator—or mine—into gear. That was awesome news. With much gesturing, words I partially understood and some ice drawings, he tried to explain to me that we needed to find the three golems whose hearts I had retrieved to awaken them.

Even before he began those explanations, I knew we would be doing that, and my fears resurfaced. I didn't know what they would be like and there were tons of them. Once I got the first ones up and running, they would expect me to retrieve the others. It made sense. With a better management of my energy reserve than this time around, although unpleasant, I could get it done. But once they no longer needed my services, what would become of me?

Will they allow me to remain in their city?

Nothing in Kai's behavior hinted they were the ungrateful type. However, experience had taught me that people had no qualms using then discarding you the minute they found something better or you no longer benefitted them. Wherever this planet was, there'd be no going home for me with our ship destroyed. As a convicted criminal, Earth wouldn't welcome me back anyway. For now though, I needed to refocus on the task at hand. There would be plenty of time to dwell on the less stellar moments of my past.

While the glowing light of the hearts... heartstones had strengthened as I approached the entrance of the magma room, the weakest one still flickered in an alarming way.

Whichever valo it belonged to wouldn't last much longer. To have him die now with his heartstone within his grasp would be horrible. I had trusted Kai so far, might as well continue.

Steeling myself, I hopped off the table to my feet. With great care, Kai gathered the heartstones still lying next to where I had been sitting and headed towards the alcoves lining the main hallway of that level. I followed in his wake, eyeing his precious cargo to see if they would react to their owners the way Kai's had to him. Sure enough, as we closed in on them, the somewhat dimmed heartstone flared up, its glow strengthening.

We came to a stop in front of a valo near the stairs going up to the third floor. He looked a smidge taller than Kai, broader and more muscular. Come to think of it, all the valos on this floor boasted bulkier bodies than Kai and the ones I had observed on the first floor upon entering the lower-city. Considering the amount of raw metal and gems which filled to the brink the multiple storage rooms on this level, I could only assume they were miners or at least did a lot of heavy lifting.

Kai handed me the two other heartstones so he could insert the one not-so-dimmed-anymore that appeared to belong to this valo. Remembering Kai's violent reaction when he reconnected with his, I took a few precautionary steps back. The heartstone settled into the valo's chest with a sucking sound followed by a series of little clicks as clawed hooks clasped all around it, locking it into place. I hadn't heard those sounds with Kai, but then he'd started screaming right away, covering them.

In this valo's case, it felt more like a revving engine. As soon as the heartstone locked into place, cue the blinding lights from both his chest and eyes. A rumbling sound resonated from his broad chest, rising in a slow crescendo. His body jerked, once, twice, then he threw his head back screaming.

Unfrozen

The awakened alien's knees buckled and Kai held him, easing him down. He trembled, grunting and shouting in horrible pain while he did the whole morphing I'd witnessed earlier. Kai spoke to him in a soothing tone. I didn't need to understand his words to read between the lines.

As his tremors receded, the awakened valo lifted his head to gaze at Kai, a look of wonder on his face. His hand rose to his chest, covering the heartstone pulsing within.

"I *resnet*..." he whispered. "I am whole *daju*."

Kai placed a hand on his friend's shoulder and gave it a squeeze. "Yes, *Garathu*, you are. We *june* are."

Standing there, staring at them, I felt both moved and awkward, like I was intruding on something personal. I shifted on my feet, wondering if I should introduce myself to the new guy or give them some space. My movement caught his eye and his head lifted up to look at me. He recoiled, a look of horror descending on his face.

My stomach dropped as his body mass and spiky ice armor grew.

"*Rakheeja! Rakheeja!*" His voice trembled with mix of fear and anger as he repeated the word the way one whispers the name of the boogeyman.

Oh shit...

Whatever that word meant, the guy looked like he'd seen a monster and couldn't decide whether to run or bash its head in—or rather bash *my* head in. I reminded him of a pretty bad something, or more likely, someone. If he went berserk on me, you'd need a sponge and bucket to pick up my remains.

My pulse picked up and a sense of dread sent cold shivers down my spine. The extent of his distress had me so tied up in knots my muscles felt on the verge of snapping. I took a few more steps back, my flight instincts yelling for me to run. Kai's head jerked towards me and he raised his palm in an arresting gesture.

"No, Lydia. Calm. Zaktaul is *Vureta*."

Zaktaul was *Vureta* all right, whatever that meant. I hesitated. While I trusted Kai, his buddy was not only bigger than he, but also appeared stronger. If he decided to come after me, I doubted Kai would be able to hold him back. However, running away might trigger predatory instincts, so once more, I silenced my impulse. Forcing myself to stand still, I watched, helpless as Kai attempted to put his friend's fears to rest.

Putting both hands on his friend's shoulders, Kai stared into his eyes.

"Calm, Zaktaul," Kai said, his tone appeasing. "*Ieru* is not *Rakheeja*. *Ieru* is *hoyna*."

"No?" Zaktaul asked before casting a menacing glance in my direction.

"No. Lydia is *hoyna*."

Although still suspicious, tension drained from Zaktaul's shoulders as he listened to Kai give him a quick rundown of my contribution to his awakening... at least so I gathered from what I heard.

"I understand," Zaktaul said, his voice doubled as Kai's had been in that morphed state.

He rose to his feet, towering over Kai's humanoid form by two heads, and leveled his glowing ice blue eyes on me.

Oh shit.

Chapter 5

KAI

How stupid of me not to have anticipated this. I should have expected his panic and anger. Only moments ago, I had experienced the same agony as my memories of my time before my heartstone was taken from me came rushing back. All the Creator had done to us came crashing down on me. Our freedom, our free will, our mortality, and even our emotions, stolen to create the perfect servants... the perfect slaves.

I was whole again and it hurt. Joy and sorrow clawed at my soul, but I couldn't dwell on my newly returned emotions. The scent of Lydia's fear permeated the room, stirring my protective instincts. I needed to reassure her. Zaktaul wouldn't harm her, not anymore. Chances were, I would have reacted in a similar fashion had I not spoken with her prior to reuniting with my heartstone. We would need to be more careful as we awakened the others.

From where I stood, my acute hearing picked up the panicked flutter of her heartbeat. Her pupils, dilated with fear, obscured the beautiful, pale blue color of her eyes, their shade identical to my skin. They were stunning and stood out against her dark complexion, the same warm brown as the highly sought after, soft and pliable, yet incredibly resilient wood from the kumeri tree. Now that I could fully appreciate it, I wanted her eyes to sparkle like they had when she enjoyed the frozen riverfruit flower.

I took a couple of steps towards her. Lydia's eyes flicked to me before latching on to my brother again. Her arms tightened around the two heartstones she still held pressed to her chest.

"Calm, Lydia," I said with my softest voice. "All is well."

I moved closer to her and she allowed it, although her fear didn't diminish.

"Lydia, meet my friend Zaktaul'dva Uur E'lek."

I couldn't help smiling when her eyes glazed over halfway through stating his name. Without her, I never would have realized how daunting our names could appear to strangers. The Strangers hadn't cringed at them. Then again, they never bothered with our names, only our skills. Most of the other valo species on Sonhadra didn't have names as complex as ours. Well, complex to those who didn't understand their structure.

"Zaktaul, please meet our rescuer, Lydia. Our names are complex to her. Will you grant her the honor of calling you Zak?"

He eyed her with curiosity.

"She fears me," Zak said, sounding surprised.

"Your battle form intimidates her. She's small with no natural defenses; no claws, no fangs, and no visible venom sacs."

"She truly is not a Creator."

"No, she isn't." I turned to Lydia who watched our conversation with growing concern and gave her a reassuring smile. "She's afraid. Will you not appease her?"

"Yes," Zak said. "She has made us both whole again. A debt is owed. The honor is mine."

I smiled at my brother and touched two fingers to my heartstone in a sign of gratitude.

He took a step forward. Lydia sucked in air and moved closer to me, seeking my protection. Although I didn't like her being distressed, in an odd way, it pleased me that she would look to me for safety.

Zak stopped and shed his battle form, returning to his normal size. The scent of Lydia's fear dimmed, and her shoulders relaxed.

"Thank you, Lydia, for returning my heartstone," Zak said, his voice booming despite his gentle tone. "It would honor me if you would call me Zak."

Lydia eyed me, uncertainty etched on her face.

I smiled. "Lydia, Kai," I said, pointing at her then me. "Lydia, Zak," I added, pointing at her then at Zak.

She heaved a sigh of relief, beamed at me then offered Zak a shy smile.

"*heloh*, Zak. *Pleez tuhmeet* you."

Zak blinked, then gave me a confused look. I tugged the right side of my mouth to express my own ignorance of her words. He pointed at the heartstones still cradled in Lydia's arms.

"Let's find their owners," he said.

I caught myself almost doing Lydia's up-down headshake and repressed a smile.

"Yes, let us proceed."

I turned to Lydia to tell her but she had already caught on. She handed me the heartstones and, with Zak in the lead, we moved forward through the remaining alcoves.

Although their glow strengthened, their owners clearly weren't on this floor. If my suspicions were accurate, each of the outer altars corresponded to a specific golem class, and therefore a specific floor. Confirming my assumption, when we reached the third floor dedicated to the Crafters like myself, neither of the remaining heartstones flared. The one for this floor had already been assigned to me. Yet, the glow of the brightest among the two heartstones increased steadily as we headed towards the stairs to the second floor.

Heavy footsteps climbing down resounded in the quiet room. Lydia moved closer to me, her warm, delicate fingers wrapping around my upper arm. The pleasant heat seeped through my skin, melting the ice inside me. It had been too long since I'd felt warmth that didn't cause discomfort. I wondered how greater contact with her would feel.

Dukeeln's tall and broad frame stepping onto the landing pulled me away from my wandering thoughts. The Builder stopped when he saw us. His gaze roamed over us, pausing ever so slightly on Lydia before locking on to the precious contents in my hands.

"My heartstone called to me," Dukeeln said with his gravelly voice, even deeper than Zak's.

My heartstone swelled with joy at the sight of another of my brothers awakened. Until now, I hadn't realized the full extent of the loneliness that crushed me from all sides. How I had missed the companionship of my people.

I made to move towards him, but Lydia's hand tightened around my arm. Of course, this new arrival would scare her. It had to be terrifying for a small, defenseless creature such as she to have so many huge valos surrounding her. Worst still, being unable to properly communicate with us had to make her feel even more isolated. Not wanting to distress her further, I stayed at her side and extended the heartstone to Zak to pass it on to our brother.

"Our friend, Lydia, retrieved some of our heartstones for us," I said.

By making him aware before reconnecting with his heartstone, I hoped to limit the risk of panic once his memory returned. This time, he stared at Lydia, examining her from head to toe. For some reason I couldn't explain, the intensity of his gaze bothered me. The urge to shove her behind me to shield her from it came over me out of nowhere. As if sensing the emotions coursing through me, Lydia shifted, moving closer still and partially hid herself behind me.

"Friend?" Dukeeln asked, his tone devoid of emotion. "Is she not the child of the Strangers? She resembles them, and yet not."

"No, she isn't," I replied as Zak presented Dukeeln with his heartstone. "I am uncertain of her species, but she faced great discomfort through the lava room to recover our heartstones and shelter them from the heat."

"Very well," Dukeeln said before inserting his heartstone into his chest.

Like Zak and I had, he suffered through the return of his memory, the pain of his losses, and years of slavery under the Creator and the Strangers. Through it, Zak supported Dukeeln while I whispered calming words to Lydia who now held onto my arm with both hands. I didn't know how many of my words she understood. My brain wasn't functioning properly, overwhelmed by the intoxicating feel of the side of her body pressed against mine.

Once he recovered, I performed the usual introductions, and Dukeeln'vir Uur A'zuk consented to have Lydia call him Duke. Together, we climbed to the second floor then summoned a frost platform to the first floor. When Lydia saw the three of us stand on it, she refused to get on, speaking at high speed in a panicked tone. Eyes wide, her chest heaving with a frantic breathing, she vehemently shook her head from side to side when I extended a hand inviting her to come to us.

My brothers' eyebrows twitched, amused by her fear of heights. Yet, even after I added the railing, she refused to get on. At first, I believed my brothers' daunting presence to be the cause but then realized she didn't trust the platform to support our combined weight. I stepped off, gave Zak the heartstone, and let them go ahead before summoning another platform for Lydia and me. She willingly came to me then. The relief and gratitude in her eyes once again awakened that strange emotion within me. Seeing to her well-being gave me an inexplicable sense of fulfillment.

The strange female fascinated me and stirred within me the urge to know more about her.

This time as we rode up, she didn't cling to the railing I had built to reassure her but stood close to me, our bare arms brushing against each other's.

I wished she'd cling to me.

We reached the first floor to find Duke and Zak already entering the circular entrance hall where the Gatherers and Hunters hibernated. Moments later, the screams of the newly awakened brother ricocheted off the walls and down the hallway to us. Lydia's steps wavered. Her shorter legs already required me to walk at a slower pace, but now we might as well be crawling.

Unfrozen

I didn't mind. In truth, it worked in our favor, granting Duke and Zak the time to update our brother about the latest events before he came face to face with Lydia. We reached the entrance of the greeting hall as the last of the agonized shouts echoed through the room. Lydia and I stayed by the doorway, watching as Zak and Duke spoke to Seibkal.

Seibkal's voice rose, pitching with agitation. Rising up in his battle form, he shifted on his feet, looking ready to charge through our brothers and bolt outside. Both Zak and Duke raised their palms in an appeasing gesture. I cast a glance at Lydia, trying to keep a neutral expression on my face.

"Stay here, Lydia. I will return."

Eyes wide, she wrapped both her hands around my arm to keep me from leaving her. My heartstone warmed at the contact. Although it pained me to leave her side, Seibkal needed me. Hunters had suffered the greatest under the wasteful ruling of the Creator. They led the rebellion against the Strangers which resulted in the loss of our heartstones. After living for centuries as unfeeling slaves, our thoughts and actions all but dictated by our maker's compulsions, this violent resurgence of emotion was traumatic.

I patted the back of Lydia's hand and gave her a reassuring smile.

"Calm, Lydia. All is well. I will return."

She hesitated, then nodded her head in agreement. "Okay," she whispered.

I gently pulled my arm out of her hands and she let them fall to her side. With one last smile, I hurried to my brothers.

"She has returned!" Seibkal shouted, his armor thickening around him. "She will bend us to her will and make monsters of us again!"

"No, Seibkal," Duke said as softly as his rumbling voice allowed. "Tarakheen has not returned. The Creator and the Stangers have not returned."

"Why did you awaken me then?" Seibkal asked, his large hand resting over his heartstone. "Why not leave me in peace?"

"You were dying, brother," Zak said. "Your heartstone was but a flicker. Too many of us have returned to Sonhadra during our slumber."

Seibkal shook his head, as if trying to come to terms with what he was hearing.

"But how did you get it? How did you cross the fire lake?"

"We had the help of a friend," I said, closing the distance with them. "A friend who will help us awaken the others so that we can rebuild our beloved city of E'lek and reform the tribes. We are free, brother. We are whole again."

Seibkal turned his head to face me, the panic in his eyes giving way to a glimmer of hope. The spiky ice armor surrounding him receded, his mass returning to normal. Relief flooded through me as I stepped up to him and placed a comforting hand on his shoulder.

"All of the others?" he breathed out. "The females?"

They would be a major problem, one I hadn't had a chance to ponder over yet, but we would find a solution.

"We'll awaken all of our brothers first and then, together, we'll figure out a way to reach the island." I put all the conviction in my voice that I could muster.

The sliver of a smile was blossoming on his face when something caught his attention over my shoulder. Seibkal recoiled, his eyes widening in horror. I turned my head to look over my shoulder. Lydia, arms wrapped around her midsection, appeared ready to take flight.

"Creator," Seibkal whispered, his voice full of dread.

My head jerked towards him. "No Seibkal. She's a friend. Not a Creator."

"You lied!" he hissed at me, his battle form resurfacing.

"Listen—"

"YOU LIED!" he thundered.

He shoved me back with his battle strength, sending me careening through the room.

"Kai!" Lydia shouted, her voice laced with fear.

I crashed against the large glow-stone altar in the center of room before I could finish summoning my own battle form. My partial armor absorbed most of the impact, but my teeth nevertheless rattled in my head. Although our *normal* bodies were more resilient since the change, we couldn't face off against a valo in battle form without breaking.

I clambered to my feet.

"I will not be enslaved again!" Seibkal yelled. "She will never control me again!"

He tried to barrel through Duke and Zak, now also in their battle forms. They tackled him to the floor but he fought them off, screaming like a wounded beast. Although not as bulky as Duke or Zak, as a Hunter, Seibkal was faster and better versed in combat. He slithered his way free of them, twisting Duke's arm to force him to let go. I raced up to him and dodged by the narrowest margin the massive fist he threw at me. Duke and Zak got back up and helped me corner him.

"Calm, Seibkal!" I shouted. "She's not a Creator. You are safe."

But even as I spoke those words, I knew the Hunter was too far gone to be reasoned with. The insanity on his face bode ill. If we didn't find a way to subdue him quickly, he could severely harm us, or worse, Lydia.

"YOU LIE! SHE CONTROLS YOU!"

"She can't control us, brother," Zak said. "She's not a Creator. Remember, we can't be controlled once united with our heartstones."

He had stopped listening. His gaze flicked between Lydia, Zak, Duke, and me. The fight seemed to drain out of him and he took two clumsy steps backwards. His eyes lost focus, their glow dimming.

"I won't go back. I won't be enslaved again," he muttered under his breath.

The armor covering his chest parted, exposing his heartstone.

"Seibkal?" I called, confused.

The madness left his features and an eerie air of peace settled there instead. The clasps of his heartstone released with a clicking sound. A sense of foreboding washed over me.

Seibkal's eyes connected with mine. "I will never be a slave again," he repeated, his tone conversational.

I knew what would happen even before he did it. He pulled the heartstone out of its socket. Zak, Duke and I rushed to stop him. Our movements seemed slow, as if underwater. He raised his hand above his head and brought it down with all his strength, smashing his heartstone against the hard, frozen stone floor. A blinding light erupted, forcing us to avert our eyes. The air charged with energy that rippled over my skin and a sharp pain stabbed my chest. Seibkal collapsed to his knees before sitting back on his haunches.

"I am free..." he whispered as the light faded from his eyes.

His eyelids closed, his shoulders drooped, and with one last heavy sigh, his chin dropped to his chest. As I stood there, watching my brother's senseless death, the stabbing sensation in my chest morphed into an open flame inside my heartstone. The lava river below flowed through my veins, burning me from the inside out as I felt Seibkal's passing.

Surrendering control to my battle form, I shouted my anguish. Duke and Zak, also morphed, merged their voices with mine, roaring with the same helpless fury. Even gone, those twice damned Creators continued to destroy my people. I wanted to run up to the upper-city and obliterate Tarakheen's statues and likenesses until nothing remained of her and the pain she had wrought upon us. In my rage, I raised my fist, bellowing as I smashed it against the floor, picturing Tarakheen's perfect face beneath it.

A high-pitched squeal made me jerk my head around, drawing Duke and Zak's attention as well. Through the red haze blurring my vision, the slim silhouette of a female stood in the doorway leading to the main hall. Hands flying to her face, she slapped them over her mouth and took shaky steps backwards, away from us.

The smell of fear wafted to us. Fear and another subtle scent below, delicate and fresh like an early winter breeze.

Lydia's...

The haze fell from my eyes.

Clamping down my sorrow, I stepped towards her, eager to reassure her that all was well. Instead, panic settled on her soft features. She raised her palms facing me, pleading, her head shaking from side to side. Water trickled from her eyes, drenching her cheeks.

"I'm sorry! I'm sorry!" she said, her voice trembling.

She turned on her heels and ran.

"Lydia!" I called out, then chased after her.

The faint sound of her heart pounding fast and hard reached my ears. I worried it might burst. The need to appease her rode me hard. The sour scent of her fear twisted my insides. She should never be afraid of me. I should be her calm. With my speed, I caught her in no time and wrapped my arms around her, careful not to squish her. Lydia screamed, the high pitch stabbing my ears. Her body trembled against mine.

I opened my mouth to soothe her but a shout of pain escaped me instead. Searing agony erupted all over my chest and arms. Steam rose to my face, forcing me to let go. Lydia took off running again, her skin pulsating with a red glow as if lava coursed right below the surface. Unable to reach the second floor without my assistance, she ran into the hot spring room—another dead-end.

Unfrozen

Her flaring up hadn't damaged me, only the outer shell of my ice armor which would heal in no time. I shouldn't have chased after her in my battle form. She'd been traumatized enough by our display of grief. But had I caught her in my normal form, I'd be covered in blisters.

The footsteps approaching from behind made me turn around.

"We do not fault her for this tragedy," Duke said.

Although I hadn't thought they would, hearing the words spoken alleviated the concern I hadn't realized lurked within.

"She thinks we do. It is best I go to her alone. She's terrified."

"Very well," Zak said. "We will tend our brother."

"Thank you," I said.

Without another word, I headed towards Lydia's hideout.

Chapter 6

LYDIA

I couldn't scream past the fear choking me. I couldn't think beyond the terror that fogged my mind. A single thought drove me: *flee*. The only way out of this underground city required me to run past them. They were too fast and would catch me in a heartbeat. Kai already had, once. That last flare up to free myself had used up all the energy I still possessed. Only adrenalin kept me going. His shout of pain lingered in my ears. It had to have enraged him further. I needed to get away, run and hide from their fury.

The sound of that valo's heartstone shattering played in a loop in my mind. My skin still crawled with the pain, the anguish that had resonated in Kai, Duke and Zak's voices as they roared with rage. The hatred and violence in their eyes when they turned toward me promised brutal retribution. Something about me had driven their brother to madness.

I darted toward the hot spring room. The temperature there didn't climb anywhere near as high as that of the lava room, but it should keep me safe from them. What I wouldn't give for an access to the lowest level. Whatever damage my flare had caused Kai, he had already recovered and his heavy footsteps pounded the floor behind me while he gave chase again.

Heart and legs pumping, I slapped my hand on the wall to help my center of gravity as I barreled into the room. Without slowing, I dove into the spring, hoping it was deep enough at that location to avoid busting my head open at the bottom. Heat enshrouded me. I almost let myself sink further. My lungs, already deprived of oxygen from my frantic escape, had different demands. Drained and weary, my limbs fought me, getting heavier with each stroke toward the surface. Cool air caressed my skin when my face breached the surface. I gulped in air with greed, then choked on the water that sneaked into my throat and airways at the same time.

"Lydia!"

Kai's voice startled me. In a panicked move to turn toward him, I sank again and swallowed more water. Chest burning, I flailed with sluggish movements, unable to muster the strength to keep my head above water.

I'm drowning!

The dreadful thought echoed in my head and my blood turned to acid from lack of oxygen. My vision darkened and my arms turned to lead. In the distance, a voice called my name.

Something cold clasped around my wrist and yanked. Weightless, I flew out of the water before colliding against a cool and hard surface. Strong arms wrapped around my back, holding me up. I coughed and sputtered, gasping for air. Too weak to move, to fight or even panic, I lay helpless in the arms of my rescuer. The warmth of the room against the chill of Kai's skin made me shiver.

"Calm, Lydia. You are safe."

His gentle voice oozed with concern. When my coughing receded, Kai brushed my wet hair off my face with his fingertips. Looking up at him through blurred vision, I opened my mouth to speak, unsure what I wanted to say, but lacked the energy to even form words. My head lolled as another shiver coursed through me. I rested my cheek against his chest and his arms tightened around me. No regular heartbeat thumped in my ear. Instead, a whooshing sound emanated from his heartstone with each pulsating glow.

Its slow, steady rhythm appeased me.

Kai lifted me in his arms and my body swayed with each of his steps out of the hot spring room. I tried to protest but only a half-coherent mumble tumbled out of my mouth.

"Calm, Lydia," Kai repeated. *"Nesuur atu sier* you."

The dimmed lighting of the hot spring room gave way to the brightness of the main hallway. Hazy silhouettes entered my line of sight; Zak and Duke. My skin tingled with the feel of weightlessness that often preceded the loss of consciousness. Having tapped out my system, I fought a losing battle against it.

"Is she *toreig*?" Duke's muffled voice asked.

Kai's response got lost in the darkness that swallowed me.

―――⧛⧚―――

I AWAKENED TO THE GENTLE droning of Kai's voice to my right. Eyes shut, I remained still, taking stock of my current situation. Beneath me, a plushy fur softened the hard surface upon which I lay on my back. The damp fabric of my ragged makeshift toga clung to my skin. That it was no longer soaking wet, despite the cooler temperature in the room, indicated I'd been out of commission for some time. My body temperature felt a great deal lower than its usual over-the-chart level. It didn't surprise me considering how today's adventures had worn me to the bone.

Unfrozen

How odd I should feel dizzy lying down. Moving felt like way too much effort, so I didn't and focused on Kai's words.

"...show you where we find them. The iwaki only blossoms in the spring. I used to love their scent before the change, so fresh and delicate. They symbolize rebirth and new beginnings. You remind me of them. That's why I made one for you this morning."

My chest tightened at being compared to the valos' symbol of life, despite what had happened with his brother. It also struck a chord with me considering I had been wrongfully accused of causing hundreds of deaths before being condemned to life on the *Concord*. All so they could experiment on me.

Based on the wistfulness of his tone, I could picture the faraway look that Kai's face probably held.

"They come in different colors. We feed their seeds to the paexi, the glowing bugs you saw in the garden yesterday. It colors the glowing resin they secrete and that's how I illuminate the patterns I carve on the walls and on the ice. The Gatherers know how to make iwakis blossom throughout the year. They've all been hibernating for so long, I've only been able to get colored resin for two moon cycles per year for the past centuries. Now, thanks to you, our gardens can thrive again through every season."

It hit me then; I'd understood every single one of his words. Since he'd first spoken to me this morning, my universal translator had been working overtime to decipher his language. The more we talked, the more words it identified. How long had Kai been at it? Was it even the same day?

Cracking my eyes open, I recognized the pattern on the ceiling as the bedroom I had previously slept in. I lifted my left shoulder to turn on my side but flopped back down. My limbs felt like jelly and my hollow stomach cramped. Chilled and clammy, my hands shook in tandem with my erratic heartbeat. I needed to eat something soon or I would go into hypoglycemic shock. It had already happened twice during Dr. Sobin's experiments. If I fell into a coma, Kai probably wouldn't have a glucose tablet or Glucagon shots handy to save me.

"Lydia!" Kai said.

At the edge of my vision, his tall frame rose from the ice bench he'd been sitting on before leaning over me. The concern on his face erased any lingering fear I held that he blamed me for his brother's death.

"F… Foo…" I mumbled, unable to form the word.

"I do not understand your words." He cast a searching glance at my body before looking back at my face. "Are you hurt?"

My stomach clenched with a pang of hunger then grumbled. Kai's head snapped towards my belly, his face brightening.

"You need sustenance. I have brought some for you," he said, waving at the table next to the bed.

The sweet scent floating around the room registered at last. My mouth watered, knowing the hard-shelled fruit lay open within reach. The ceiling spun when I lifted my head. I closed my eyes and rested it back on my pillow.

"I'll help you, Lydia."

Kai's strong arms slipped under me, lifting me up like I weighed nothing. He sat down on the bed and cradled me on his lap. Cheek pressed against his shoulder, I reopened my eyes to see a few slices of the fish I had eaten earlier, the sweet fruit Kai had made ice cream with, and a stack of little red cubes.

"Start with the gurahn cubes," Kai said. "Zak made them for you. You don't have to chew. Let them melt on your tongue."

Bless your heart!

Some juice overloaded with sugar would have been ideal right now, but I'd take anything I could get. Kai reached for one of the small cubes and pushed it between my parted lips. The sweet taste of candied apple exploded in my mouth. I sucked with greed on the frozen cube which melted into a creamy texture on my tongue. Kai's rumbling chuckle against my side made me realized I'd moaned with pleasure. I swallowed and opened again for the next cube he held ready for me. Piece by piece, he fed me the two dozen cubes under my stomach's impatient groans.

He didn't speak while I ate, a contented smile stretching his lips.

By the time the last one disappeared down my gullet, I no longer shook or felt dizzy. I was still weary to the bone though. As much as the fish filets called to me, I wouldn't risk flaring up, even if only my hands, to thaw them. When Kai extended his hand towards one, I shook my head.

"No. I'll have the fruit instead, please."

His hand still hovering over the fish steaks, he turned to look at me with a questioning expression on his face.

"Do you not like them?" he asked.

I chewed my bottom lip. Although he had saved me from drowning and was taking care of me, revealing the extent of my vulnerabilities sounded like a bad idea.

"Yes, I like them. But for now, I'd rather go with the fruit."

The angular lines of his face looked even sharper as he stared at me, his crystallized brows drawn into a frown. I could see his wheels turning, the way his eyes glowed and how he pursed that plump lower lip of his.

It struck me then that every parcel of his cool body surrounded me, his face only a hair's breadth from mine. With him wearing nothing but a loincloth, and me in my own barely there toga, we were skin to skin almost everywhere we touched. It felt nice. Very nice. Heat crept up my cheek at the unexpected intimacy and at the butterflies that took flight in my belly.

"You are too weakened to warm the fish," Kai said.

What?

It took me a moment to bring my wandering mind back to the topic at hand. Kai's astute deduction doused my inappropriate musings.

"Yes," I admitted with reluctance. "It takes a lot of energy to flare up or freeze. I have to use it wisely."

He nodded in that quirky way of his. "I saw you falter below, weakening with every step. Had you fallen further away, I couldn't have aided you."

The distraught look on his face stirred something within me that had lain dormant for far too long. Very few people had shown me any kind of care lately. Even before my condemnation, friends and family had distanced themselves from me. I couldn't blame them and even encouraged the few of my family who wouldn't abandon me to do so when it became clear I would be the scapegoat. The stigma from guilt by association would have destroyed their lives.

Quinn, Petra and Zoya had been my lifeline once I landed on that wretched penitentiary, even though they separated us all too soon. Once again, I wondered if any of them made it out and if we would ever meet again. My money was on Quinn. Her crazy Dr. Craig had tried to make her immortal or something along those lines by making her able to heal through anything. My own scientist told me Craig had succeeded at last. It was therefore fair to assume Quinn would have survived the crash or at least healed through it.

Would Kai help me search for her?

I smiled. "I'm fine. You got me out in time."

Twice.

"It wouldn't have been a problem had I not wasted so much energy earlier drying my toga and exploring the cave."

He harrumphed his agreement but didn't appear fully convinced. Kai grabbed a half of the hard-shell fruit and held it in his left hand, with his arm wrapped around me.

"What do you call that fruit?" I asked, pointing at it with my chin.

"It's a riverfruit."

His chest vibrated against me when he said that word, making my skin tingle. The way Kai rolled his r's reminded me of a purring cat. It was sexy as hell.

"How come we understand each other so well now?" I asked to distract myself from those sexy thoughts and out of genuine curiosity.

Kai raised his free hand and caressed the back of my left ear with two fingers. "I spoke to your device."

Goosebumps erupted all over me while a swarm of butterflies played catch in my stomach. I hadn't expected his touch to be this soft.

Kai's lips parted, the glow of his eyes intensifying as he looked at my skin.

"It's okay," I said. "It happens sometimes with my species."

Especially when sitting half-naked on an even more naked sexy alien who touches me the way you just did.

His right eyebrow twitched, and Kai looked like he wanted to touch my skin to feel the bumps. My throat tightened in anticipation and the butterflies went into overdrive. He raised his hand but rather than touching me, he waved his fingers and a white swirl of frost clouded them before firming into a spoon of ice.

I cleared my throat to hide my disappointment.

"How... How did you know I have a translation device there?" I asked.

He smiled. "You've tapped there several times this morning after I spoke and my words confused you. But the more we talked, the more you seemed to understand me. Since you were unconscious a long time, I decided to talk to your device, so it would learn my language."

Sweet, sexy, and smart. This alien is a keeper.

But something still didn't add up.

"How long was I out that you've got my translator up to speed?"

Kai tilted his head, brows drawn. "Out?" he asked.

"Unconscious."

"Oh. At least four hours."

Woah... okay.

But did we measure time the same way? Not that it really mattered right now, but still...

"And you talked to me the whole time?"

"Yes. I told you of the creation of Sonhadra four times, described the many valos species twice, explained the process of ice, wood, and stone sculpting, the best practices to illuminate carvings, as well as the care and feeding of the paexi. That's when you awakened."

I blinked.

"Didn't you get tired?"

He looked baffled by the question. "No. I could have gone on for days. I haven't talked to anyone in a long time and it was useful."

Kai looked so innocent I once again fought the urge to hug him.

"Yes, it was. I'm glad you had the patience for it. Thank you!"

He smiled and his heartstone glowed brighter.

Is he blushing?

That thought made me feel warmer.

"But, how do you understand me? I mean, you taught my translator your language, but that didn't teach you mine."

"I don't know yours," Kai said, matter-of-fact. "You are speaking mine, and your accent is delightful."

My jaw dropped, then my ears burned. I never knew that. Back on Earth, most people had translators. I always assumed we spoke in our respective languages. Maybe we did, but I compensated here since he couldn't speak mine.

"Thank you," I said, feeling self-conscious.

My gaze fell on the riverfruit he still held in his hand. Kai had prepared it differently than yesterday. The gooey, white flesh had once again been stirred but this time, he'd mixed in some red berries—probably the same ones used in those frozen cubes I ate—and something else, darker, resembling nuts. Noting what had drawn my attention, Kai scooped a spoonful and fed it to me. Although I had regained enough strength to do it myself, I couldn't pass up getting pampered.

Getting pampered or having his muscular body wrapped all around you?

In all honesty, it was both. The last year, between my trial and incarceration aboard the *Concord*, had taught me to cherish every moment of happiness or comfort that came my way. It took very little to turn your life upside-down or snuff it out completely. I couldn't begin to imagine what the future held for me. In the last handful of days, I'd been experimented on, crash-landed on some mysterious planet, escaped the fire that killed the medical crew, got hunted by a rabid family of giant, tree-hugging bugs, survived an acute case of food poisoning and falling down a big ass waterfall, AND barely avoided drowning—twice. So yes, I intended to *carpe diem* the heck out of every moment.

That first bite brought me right back to the here and now. My eyes widened as the mango-papaya-honey flavor blossomed on my tongue, spiked with chewy candied apple and crunchy roasted walnuts. It was orgasmic.

"This is sooooooo good!" I moaned with my mouth full.

Kai grinned, revealing pearly white, razor sharp teeth I hadn't noticed before. I swallowed without finishing chewing. The food got stuck in my throat before painfully resuming its way down to my stomach. The absurd thought that he was fattening me to eat me later wouldn't leave me alone now that it had entered my mind.

His smile faded and he tilted his head to the side at my sudden change of mood.

"You're not going to eat me with those are you?" I asked, my fingers fiddling with the ragged edge of my toga.

He blinked.

"Those what?" Kai asked. "And no, valos do not eat anymore since the change. And before that, we didn't eat people. Why would you think that?"

I shifted on his lap, wondering how honest I should be.

"It's just that… you have really sharp teeth," I said in a small voice.

He chuckled, his eyes widening in disbelief. "And you have very blunt teeth, like plant eaters. Yet, do you not enjoy fish and maybe even meat too?"

I nodded, my ears burning with embarrassment.

"Should I fear you will try to eat my brothers and me?"

I made a face at him, his gentle, mocking tone reassuring me that he was teasing.

"Maybe someday. For now, I will stick with the fish and riverfruit," I said in the same tone, hoping he would understand it was a joke.

Kai's smile broadened. It did weird and delicious things to me.

"But... how do you survive if you don't eat?" I asked. "You don't feel like a machine."

Can I stick my foot any deeper?

Kai's sharp features softened and his right eyebrow twitched again. I wondered if it was a sign of amusement. As he scooped more of the fruit mixture and brought it to my lips, I noticed for the first time that his fingers, while similar to mine, didn't have nails. Eager to keep myself from speaking out of turn again, I welcomed the spoonful, enjoying the crunchiness of the nuts.

"Before the change, my people ate fruits, meat, fish, vegetables, grains, and more prepared in all kinds of wondrous ways," he said in a wistful voice. "As valos, we no longer require traditional sustenance. For us, the Northern Valos, the sun provides our greatest source of energy. In its absence, we absorb nutrients and moisture directly from the air. But we can survive for extended periods without the sun."

As he spoke, Kai continued to feed me.

"My brothers in their alcoves have gone into hibernation. In that state, our bodies require minimal resources to function. So, the air provides more than enough to sustain us for decades, even centuries."

I opened my mouth to ask a question but thought better of it.

Kai narrowed his eyes at me. I hadn't fooled him.

Unfrozen

"You wanted to ask why some of them have died then, am I right?"

My cheeks heated and I nodded, uncomfortable. This felt like too sensitive a topic after what had happened earlier.

"They died because they lost the will to live," Kai said, pain creeping into his voice.

The glow of his eyes intensified as they locked with mine. His expression, grave and solemn, held infinite sorrow.

"What happened to Seibkal is not your fault."

Air rushed out of me. Until this moment, I hadn't realized how much I had needed to hear him say those words. I didn't think myself responsible but something about me had sent that poor valo over the edge, and I wanted to understand what.

"Eat, Lydia. All is well."

I opened my mouth to receive another mouthful.

"The Creator destroyed everything we were," Kai said with a mix of anger and sadness. "Under her command, the Strangers changed us, turned us into valos, and enslaved us. They had no respect for life or the balance of nature. They came and took without care for the consequences."

A growl entered his voice while his face hardened.

"We revolted, fought back, but they had powers we couldn't combat. They ripped out our heartstones, stealing our free will, our emotions, our pride. They made us no more than obedient puppets."

Kai all but spat out those last words. My heart squeezed as sharp ice spikes peeked out of his arms and shoulders in response to his emotions.

"One day, they left without a word. We lingered without feelings, going through the routine they had given us until there were no more gems or ore to be mined, and the uneaten crops rotted away in storage. Without a purpose, my brothers were losing their minds, so they went to sleep, waiting for the Creator to return. But she never did."

That explained so much and yet raised so many questions. How horrible it must have been over all those years to watch, helpless, as one by one, his brothers gave up waiting and their lights faded. In a way, not having his heartstone had been a blessing in disguise so he didn't feel the pain of their loss. I wanted to hug Kai and comfort him, but I didn't know if he would welcome the gesture.

"The Creator and the Strangers... Who were they? Where did they come from?" I asked.

"We don't really know. One day, they came from the sky. We welcomed them as guests, opened our homes to them, fed and sheltered the handful of them who chose not to sleep on their ships."

His brow creased and a nerve ticked at his temple, next to the fanned-fin of his ear.

"For days, they dwelled among us, studying everything, even us. They claimed it was scientific research to bring back tales of the wonders of Sonhadra back to their people once they left. And then one day, our people didn't return from hunting. We sent out rescue parties, they didn't return either."

Kai heaved a sigh, jaw clenched as he reminisced the events. Him raising another spoon to my mouth reminded me to eat. The abuse they'd faced had dampened my legendary appetite. The smooth texture of the iced treat now felt slimy in my throat, but I forced myself to swallow. My body needed the fuel to recover from my recent overexertion.

"The next morning, we were supposed to all go as a single group instead of the small parties that kept disappearing. Except, we woke up to find ourselves strapped aboard the Strangers' ships while they performed horrible experiments on us. I can still hear the screams of my people. We hadn't realized that they had already begun experimenting on the nomad tribes of the Northern Valos."

"Nomads?" I asked.

"My people are divided into five tribes," Kai explained. "This is our main city, E'lek, which binds us all. The four other tribes, O'Tuk, I'Xol, A'zuk to which Duke belongs, and U'Gar to which Seibkal belonged, were all nomadic. They provided E'lek with the resources otherwise not available near the city. We transformed them into refined goods for trade with other valos cities. Two to three moon cycles could pass without us seeing them, so we didn't question their absence."

That made sense. Standard predatory behavior; target the isolated prey first to thin the herd.

"By the time they were done, they had granted us the gift of frost and immortality, but taken away our freedom, and later our free will."

"You retained your free will at first?" I asked, as he fed me the last scoop from the first half of the fruit.

"Yes. We were as I am now, with feelings, memories of our past and independent thoughts. The Strangers could bend us to their will with a device attached to their wrists. It caused terrible pain when we disobeyed or challenged them." He looked at me, as if wanting to drive home the extent of their suffering. "It felt like our heartstone would combust in our chests. Tarakheen though, the Creator, didn't use a device that we could see. Yet, with one look, she could drop us all to our knees."

Kai put the empty shell on the table but this time I pointed to the fish. He eyed me with a confused look.

Yes, sweetheart, a girl is allowed to change her mind.

It wasn't so much that I had changed my mind but between the melting cubes and that first half of the fruit, I'd regained enough strength to thaw the fish steaks without hurting myself. I could also use the protein and iron. And, damn it, those things were super tasty! In all the tragedies that had befallen me, my high metabolism was my greatest blessing. The way I loved food, they'd need a towing machine to cart me around.

Or a big ice elemental...

Kai handed me one of the fish steaks which I all but yanked out of his grasp in my greed.

"Please continue," I said, thawing the first piece.

His lips stretched into an amused smile.

"Tarakheen wanted the resources found in this cave, mainly the xorkeb ore which she believed held special properties and our arwal gems, although only the green ones. So, the Strangers chased us from the upper-city, which we had to adapt to their needs, and this cave became our home. It expanded as we mined it for them. Every two moons, one of their vessels would come and we would load it with a new shipment."

Having all but inhaled that first fish steak, I eyed the remaining stack of four. Before I could ask, Kai reached with his long arm and handed me another piece.

"So why did they leave? If the ore and gems were precious enough to sacrifice an entire population, why leave all of that behind?" I asked.

I didn't know if the ore would be of value on Earth, but I bet the gems would be. With the amount they had stashed below, I could probably buy every country in the world.

"We do not know that either," Kai said, a somber expression on his face. "Maybe we had provided them with the quantities they needed. Maybe they found something better elsewhere. Before you came, a part of me wanted them to return so that my brothers would awaken instead of dying in their sleep. Yet, another part of me thought maybe death was better than slavery."

My chest constricted at the raw emotion that crossed his features. He looked at me with wonder, as if he couldn't believe I was real.

"Now, I hope they never return," he whispered, his heartstone glowing fierce. "You are our iwaki, our rebirth, the promise of new life."

STOMACH BULGING FROM overindulgence, I padded along next to Kai on our way to the upper-city. After my meal, and with much embarrassment, I'd expressed my urgent need of using the toilet. He appeared even more embarrassed, not by the topic, but for not having thought of it sooner himself. Nothing warranted his guilt. After centuries of relying exclusively on sun and moisture in the air for his survival, basic bodily functions were bound to be light-years away from his mind.

The lower-city contained no bathroom, kitchen or recreational area. Having no use for them, the valos hadn't bothered building them as more space became available through their mining efforts. Since they didn't eat or sleep, I wondered why they had bedrooms but decided to steer clear of that touchy topic. Kai believed the upper-city dwellings of the Strangers would provide everything I needed but food. We emerged onto the main hallway from the winding corridor leading to the bedrooms and almost smashed into Duke. He had also been turning the corner, coming from the opposite direction, his hands burdened with a large wooden crate.

On instinct, I jumped a couple of steps back, ready to run.

Despite being back to his normal form and the absence of aggression on his features, Duke's broad shoulders, bulky arms, and towering height intimidated me. The crystals of his right eyebrow twitched, like Kai's had done earlier.

Is he laughing at me?

"The female is even more skittish than a wild sekubu," Duke said, sounding amused. "You must tell her not to fear me. I wish her no harm. In fact, I come bearing gifts."

That got my attention.

"Gifts?" I asked, before Kai could respond. "You brought me gifts?"

Eyes latched onto the container in Duke's hands, I leaned forward, half hiding behind Kai's right shoulder. Like everything else in E'Lek, flourishing swirls adorned the chest, with some of the patterns illuminated with the glowing resin Kai had mentioned earlier. It looked dim in comparison to the illuminations here. I could only surmise it had been built a long time ago.

Duke recoiled in surprise, his large eyes widening further. "You speak our words!"

Unfrozen

Kai's chest swelled, a smug look settling on his sharp features. It was cute, like a kid proudly showing off his accomplishment to a sibling.

"I taught our language to Lydia's speech device while she rested."

"Well done, Qaezul," Duke said, laying his burden on the floor.

Antsy with curiosity, I took a step forward. Duke pressed his thumb against one of the swirling patterns on the cover. It depressed, revealing the concealed opening mechanism. The lid parted in two, sliding open, and then each half folded against the sides. I stretched my neck to look inside. Two piles of neatly folded, colorful fabric filled the chest to the brim.

Oh God! Could it be?

Duke picked up an ice-blue fabric with glowing, white, linear patterns. He held it up before me, letting it unravel. I squealed at the sight of the flowy, long-sleeve tunic with a round neck. Jumping on the balls of my feet, I clapped my hands with excitement. The remaining shreds of my *toga* were a couple of days away from disintegrating right off my back. A surgery blanket had never been intended to serve as survival clothing.

All fears forgotten, I raced over to Duke who extended the tunic towards me. I grabbed it and held it stretched against my chest to check the fit. Whoever it had belonged to must have been mighty tall. The hem almost reached my knees and the sleeves appeared too long by at least two hands.

I couldn't care less.

Clean clothes!

And the fabric... I lifted the sleeve to my face and rubbed it against my cheek. The softness of cashmere caressed my skin, even where the resin colored the tunic. Although luxurious, the material didn't feel flimsy or delicate, but as sturdy as suede.

Overwhelmed with gratitude I looked up at Duke's bemused face and smacked a kiss on his cheek.

"Thank you!"

I twirled, the tunic still pressed against me. My bladder put a hard stop to my enthusiasm. The sudden movement reminded me the dam would burst any minute now, with or without my consent. My fist tightened on the tunic and I slammed my legs closed, holding them shut for fear of making a mess. I cast a panicked look at Kai who stared back at me, his jaw clenched and his normally plump lower lip tightened into a thin line. His reaction confused me.

"Something wrong?" Duke asked.

"I gotta pee!" I ground out through my teeth.

Nonplussed, Duke tilted his head. "You need to what?"

"She needs to urinate," Kai said in a clipped tone. "I was taking her to the hygiene facilities."

Oh God...

Why did the proper term make it so much more embarrassing?

"I see," Duke said. He closed the lid of the chest and pushed it against the wall, then jerked his head toward the entrance. "This way."

Cheeks and ears burning, I followed, waddling like a duck. As I walked, the pressure lessened, giving me a temporary reprieve and I hastened the pace. A couple of times, my stomach cramped, forcing me to stop, eyes and legs shut tight as I battled against the urge to just let go. When we entered the circular entrance hall, I couldn't resist casting a glance at the alcove where the guys had awakened Seibkal. It stood empty. I averted my eyes and didn't ask what they had done with him.

Crisp, clean air kissed my skin when we emerged from the lower-city and approached the stairs. The first step made me realize the impossible task laid before me. Raising my foot to climb the first one had me doubling over, certain this time I would mess myself. Teeth clenched, hands fisting the tunic I still held, I fought the burn of my overflowing bladder.

Duke, standing a few steps ahead, turned around and looked at me, his right eyebrow twitching. I wanted to punch the smug bastard.

"I will help you," he said, climbing back down.

The laughter in his voice irked me, but I kept my mouth shut, too grateful for his assistance.

"I have her," Kai snapped, startling both Duke and me.

Duke dropped the arms he'd extended toward me while Kai's slipped behind my knees and back, lifting me up like a bride. He didn't look at me or Duke and climbed the stairs like he wanted to squash them underfoot.

Oh shit! He's jealous!

I bit the inside of my cheeks to keep myself from grinning and immediately felt horrible about it. His possessiveness tickled me pink. Who didn't like being wanted, especially by someone that hot and sweet? However, I didn't want to be the cause of drama between them. That kiss on

Duke's cheek had been innocent and a spur of the moment thing. But Kai had reasons to be upset. Over the past two days, he'd fed me, saved me twice, taught me their language, and looked after me. I couldn't even recall saying, 'thank you' more than once to him. Then his brother comes along, flashes a nice piece of clothing in front of me, and I'm all over him. Although I hadn't meant it like that, I could see how perceptions could be misleading.

Duke gave Kai an assessing glance then followed without a word. I hadn't perceived any romantic interest from Duke. Despite his badass appearance, he struck me as a teddy bear with a big sense of humor lurking beneath the surface. The typical big brother who took pleasure in pulling on his baby sister's pigtails but would bring her ice cream in apology if one of his jokes went too far.

As we reached the landing, the rays of the sun found my exposed skin despite the fading light of late afternoon. Kai didn't set me down as I would have expected, but kept trudging on toward the upper city.

Wanting to break the uncomfortable silence, I pointed at the tall female statue at the entrance of the city.

"Is that Tara...? Hmm... Sorry, I forget her name."

"Yes," Kai said. "That is Tarakheen, our Creator. As you can see," he said, jerking his chin toward the city, "she loved herself very much."

Even in the dark of night upon first entering the city, I had noticed the numerous carvings representing her. In the light of day, the abandoned state of the upper-city was even more glaring. The shadows had hidden the amount of accumulated snow, icicles, and debris blown in by the wind. However, someone—probably Duke—had cleared a path to one of the big mansions, and partially cleared its façade of the ice and frost covering its carvings. A masculine face of a similar race as Tarakheen's graced a cameo above the main entrance.

I'd come to the conclusion that Tarakheen had been some kind of expedition leader and the Strangers had been her crew or staff. From the sound of it, multiple such teams had landed throughout Sonhadra, with their respective leaders becoming the *Creator* to the other tribes or races that inhabited the planet. If I understood correctly, Kai's people were the only ones with frost powers. Other valos had been transformed to manipulate a different element, like fire, air, water, etc.

"Did you carve all this?" I asked, waving at the adornments.

"Yes," Kai said, a sliver a pride creeping into voice. "On all of these buildings and the interior as well."

"It's stunning," I said.

He smiled, tension finally leaving his features, and his hold tightened around me.

Genuine awe, not the desire to placate him, prompted that confession. The finesse and precision of each line on such a large and hard stone surface left me speechless. This wasn't like plasterwork where if you broke off a bit too much you could add more plaster and fix it. Once you broke off the stone, that was it.

Duke took the lead. Although this clearly was the entrance, the door had no handle and no visible lock or opening mechanism. The Builder valo walked up to the door and pressed his fingers against the seamless pattern of the wall by the doorframe. Like with the chest, a section of the wall, the size of a small brick, depressed and the large door slid open with a subtle sound. For some reason, I had expected the heavy, grinding growl of rock against rock.

As Kai carried me over the threshold, I glanced at the wall where Duke had activated the opening mechanism. It had returned to its default state. Had I not seen him do it, I wouldn't believe a switch hid somewhere in the pattern.

The door swished close behind us. A large hall, similar to the one in the lower-city, greeted us. A smaller version of the glow stone altar covered with elaborate carvings sat in the center. Here, no golem alcoves lined the walls. Beyond, a square living area branched off into two corridors on each side. Ahead, an elevated dais appeared to hide another section. The house was entirely made of that white stone, even the floor, although it seemed to have been treated and polished to look like quartz.

I didn't have time to take in every detail as Kai walked me through the minimalist décor with a strong Zen vibe. Unlike the lower-city, plush cushions in colorful patterns covered the hard surfaces of the stone and wooden seating. Clean in its design, the living area was elegant, stripped of unnecessary trinkets, yet mesmerizing with the subtle glowing carvings.

We followed Duke through the left corridor, both males' heavy steps echoing through the room. He stopped in front of the wall, drawing my attention to the carving. Two trees, bending toward each other as two lovers, intertwined their limbs, forming a perfect arch. I could almost feel the longing for greater closeness between the trees. My gaze shifted to Kai. Had he made these? Was this dedicated to someone who had been dear to him?

Once again, Duke touched a seemingly inconspicuous section of the wall and an arched doorway slid open. A small glow stone on a pedestal at the entrance bathed the room in a dim light. Duke ran his hand over it and the glow intensified to a more comfortable level.

Kai put me down. Confused, I looked around the empty rectangular room and cast a questioning glance at him. He, in turn, frowned at Duke.

He doesn't know either.

Of course, that made sense. As a Builder, Duke would know the ins and outs of the houses inner workings. As an artist, Kai wouldn't have such knowledge, especially for things he had no use for.

Duke touched another pattern in the wall. A panel slid open and a rounded sink came out of the wall at an odd height. I'd have to hunch down a little to wash my hands in the water that started pouring in. Next to the sink, a stack of thin towels sat on a shelf, and under it, a hole gaped at me. I assumed it was some kind of waste basket.

Moving to the side wall, Duke depressed another hidden switch. A larger panel revealed a mirror and beneath it, a wider, rectangular sink came out at the height of my breasts. My jaw dropped realizing the small sink was in fact the toilet.

How freaking tall were those Strangers?

"Press here when you are done," Duke said, indicating an otherwise unremarkable section of wall above the glow stone by the entrance. "We will wait outside."

Both males exited. The door slid shut, once more forming a seamless pattern. Had he not shown me where to press to reopen it, I'd be hyperventilating right now.

I placed the tunic on the counter by the sink. The minute I turned back to the *toilet*, my bladder roared at me with a vengeance. With much struggling and teeth grinding, I managed to find relief without making a mess. By the time I finished, I'd put Niagara Falls to shame. I wiped with one of the small towels on the shelf and discarded it in the bin. Thankfully, the toilet auto-flushed. It would have been awkward having to call Duke back in to show me how. I sauntered over to the sink then stood on my tippy-toes to wash my hands.

The girl in the mirror made me cringe. My face looked emaciated, my lips chapped, and my long, curly afro hair puffed like giant nuclear mushrooms had gone off wherever it escaped my single French braid. To think this was the image Kai had of me.

For a second, I considered using one of the bigger towels by the sink to wash and put on the tunic but thought better of it. If they had this state-of-the-art toilet, for sure they had some crazy bath somewhere. Worst case scenario, I could bathe in the hot spring in the lower-city.

I pressed the tile Duke had indicated and the door opened, revealing the two valos waiting for me.

"Better?" Kai asked.

"*Much* better," I said, with a huge grin. "Thanks, both of you."

"It is nothing," Duke said.

His gaze dropped to the tunic still held in my hand and his crystalline eyebrows drew together ever so slightly.

"I would like to bathe before wearing it," I said in response to his unspoken question. "Is there a bath here?"

"Of course," Duke said.

Unfrozen

He turned and headed down the hallway. We passed a couple more tree patterns which I guessed hid other rooms. As he approached the end of the corridor, the entire back wall slid open without any input from him.

My jaw dropped at the sight of the roman bathhouse sprawling before me.

Unlike the rough-edged hot spring in the lower-city, perfectly straight-lined, white stone encased this one. Chiseled columns rose to the ceiling on each side of the fifteen-meter pool. Glow stones embedded in the center of stylized flower patterns on the walls provided a mixed white and blue ambient light. The giant iwaki carved into the ceiling above the pool drew my eyes. The same glow stones formed its pistils while golden resin outlined the indented petals.

Duke touched a flower pattern on the first pillar by the pool. A panel slid open revealing different jars of colorful spheres the size of giant pearls. They were divided by color on the top shelf. Neatly folded towels and body cloths filled the bottom shelf. He picked a set of white and blue pearls and dropped them in the water. A fresh, fruity fragrance wafted past us.

Sneaking behind Duke, Kai grabbed a towel and body cloth and brought them to me. I bit the interior of my cheeks again to repress a smile. He didn't need to try so hard to make himself useful to me. Duke still showed no indication he wanted to enter any kind of competition over me, and even if he did, Kai would still remain my favorite.

"Thank you, Kai." I beamed at him while accepting the towels. "Thank you too, Duke," I said looking over Kai's shoulder at him.

I walked to one of the long stone benches by the pool and placed the tunic and towels on top. Lifting my head, I stared at the two valos who stood side by side at the head of the pool, watching me. I shifted, feeling awkward.

"Well, hmmm, I won't be too long."

"Take all the time you need, Lydia," Kai said, smiling. "I will wait for you."

Neither of them moved. I blinked, my underlying message having eluded them. When I still didn't get into the water, Duke tilted his head, the movement reminding me of a bird.

"Do you require something else?" Duke asked.

My fingers fiddled with the fabric of my makeshift toga and I cleared my throat.

"No, thank you. I don't need anything else," I said, my voice hesitant. "You can both go about your other duties. I'll come find you when I'm done."

Kai's heartstone flared, the way it always did when he felt strong emotions.

"You wish me to leave?" he asked.

I couldn't tell if he sounded more surprised or hurt.

"What if you require assistance during your bath?" he continued. "What if you become indisposed?"

"I will be fine," I said, softening the rejection with a smile. "I'm well fed and well rested right now, thanks to you."

Although some tension bled from his shoulders, the frown marring his bald forehead indicated he didn't quite want to drop the issue.

"It is not appropriate in my culture to undress before others," I said, my skin heating with embarrassment.

Unfrozen

Both Kai and Duke's crystalline eyebrows shot up and their eyes glowed. Had I not been feeling so self-conscious, I probably would have burst out laughing.

"Why?" Duke asked.

I shrugged and twisted the hem of my toga hard enough for a piece to tear off.

"It's our way. You only undress in front of your life partner."

Kai and Duke exchanged a look, their right eyebrows twitching. I didn't need to read minds to know they thought me strange.

"You cover your private parts too," I said, my tone defensive as I pointed at their loincloth.

"We wear them for adornment and convenience," Duke said, sticking his fingers in hidden pockets I had not noticed before. "We will wait outside then."

His mocking tone set my teeth on edge but I responded with a grateful smile.

"Thank you. I will be quick."

Kai pinched his lips and followed his brother out with obvious reluctance. Considering how I'd been streaking around for months in front of Dr. Sobin, the medical staff, and the guards on the *Concord*, my prudish behavior now seemed a little contrived. Funny thing is, I wouldn't have cared if Duke or Zak had been in the room. Kai made me self-conscious. Should he ever see me naked—and I actually hoped he would someday—it wouldn't be with me looking this ragged.

I slipped into the divinely warm and fragrant water and went to work scrubbing my skin and unknotting the bird's nest on my head.

Chapter 7

KAI

What was wrong with me? Reconnecting with my heartstone had turned me into an emotional wreck. The Valos were a peaceful people. We didn't fight each other and kept rivalries to friendly challenges. Duke's gaze upon Lydia held no covetous edge. His kindness toward her followed our customs of hospitality. Yet, the attention she bestowed upon him bothered me to no end. An irrational aggression had robbed me of coherent thought the minute Lydia's lips had connected with his cheek. I'd recognized it as a mere sign of gratitude but it still made my heartstone burn. Her current coverings looked pitiful. I should have thought of it first.

Duke's rippling muscles played under the ice-blue skin of his strong back as he marched toward the living area. Almost as bulky as Miners, Builders like Duke developed muscular bodies. I remembered all too well how Lydia's eyes had scrutinized my brother. For the first time in my existence, I felt inadequate. As an artist, I could make pretty things for her, but Builders were better suited to provide the exotic female with convenience and comfort. Gatherers and Hunters could supply a greater diversity of food and meal preparations. And there was no question Lydia loved food.

The memory of her warm skin against mine as I fed her awakened sensations beneath my loincloth I had long forgotten. Who could have imagined I'd ever welcome again anything other than frost? Yet, the heat of her body had seeped into mine, melting the ice that ran through my veins. Her softness made my fingers itch with need, especially those ridiculous bumps that had risen all over her. Lydia's pliable curves nestled perfectly with mine. I wished that meal had never ended so that she'd remain on my lap, in my embrace, forever. Remembering the sounds of pleasure she made while eating fanned the fire in my belly.

What would it feel like for her to press her lips to my cheek as well? What would it be like to have her entirely naked, pressed against my own bare flesh?

What does she look like beneath those rags?

Her shyness at exposing herself made my brows twitch. Why hide? Showing her legs, arms, and face didn't seem to bother her. What could be so special about her torso and groin that it should remain covered?

An unpleasant thought crossed my mind. Her breasts were big, swelling under her coverings. Our females' chests only inflated when with child or during their nursing years. By their size, and considering Lydia's flat belly, no babe grew inside her. Did she have offspring somewhere desperate for the return of their mother?

Duke came to a halt in the middle of the living area then turned to face me. His serious expression put a damper on my thoughts.

"The female is strange, but clearly not a Creator. Has she told you where she came from and what brought her here?"

I ran a hand over the braid at the back of my head, my heartstone heating with embarrassment. Lydia and I had talked a number of times now, but I'd learned very little about her. Eager to please her, I'd done most of the talking, spilling a lot about us.

I cleared my throat. "No. We couldn't communicate well enough for that. I explained to her what the Creator had done and only part of the reason why she took away our heartstones."

He narrowed his eyes at me. "Part?"

"She doesn't know about our females."

Duke pursed his lips, his bulging arms crossing over his chest.

"Do you believe she might be a threat to them?"

I recoiled and shook my head from side to side. "No. I am certain she wouldn't harm our females. But until we've found a way to access the island, there's no point burdening her with that knowledge."

Duke tilted his head and sucked in his bottom lip in his typical baffled expression.

"What?" I asked.

"What's wrong with your neck?"

I blinked. "Nothing's wrong. Why?"

"Why did you do that?" Duke asked, shaking his head sideways.

Really?

My heartstone heated again. I'd never imagined myself so easy to influence.

"A habit I've picked up from Lydia. Her people express negation with that gesture and agreement by shaking their heads up and down like this," I said, nodding my head the way she did.

Duke's eyebrow twitched. Mine followed suit. It had been too long since we'd had cause to be merry.

"Your female is strange. Very strange."

My female.

She wasn't mine, but I liked the sound of that, and in particular that he perceived her as such. I didn't correct him. His knowing smiled indicated he wasn't fooled.

"Yes, she is. It is refreshing."

The amusement faded from Duke's face and I braced for what would follow.

"After her bath, Lydia must go retrieve more heartstones," he said.

My spine stiffened at the finality of his tone.

"She's not our slave to be ordered about," I said, my voice clipped. "That first trip drained her."

The lines of his square jaw hardened as did his gaze.

"This has nothing to do with enslaving her. The first trip may have tired her but she looks well-rested enough now."

"She'll be even better rested in the morning."

"Our brothers don't have until morning," Duke snapped. "I went back down while Lydia slept. Even from the entrance, I can see many heartstones flickering, more than before her rest cycle. By the next sunrise, they will be dead. She *must* go back, even at the risk of her discomfort."

Fist clenched, I turned away from him and stared through the frosted side windows at the deserted plaza outside. His words held an undeniable truth. I'd seen it with my own eyes when she'd retrieved our heartstones. But I'd also seen how she'd stumbled through the last stretch, drained to the point of collapse. Even without my heartstone, I had felt a sliver of fear... for her. Now that the full range of my emotions had been restored, dread twisted my insides that something bad would happen.

Still, I couldn't let my brothers die. Lydia said it wouldn't be too bad if she didn't waste energy beforehand.

I heaved a sigh and looked at him over my shoulder.

"You are right. The flickering ones need to be retrieved in all haste. I will speak to her but we must take care. If we push her too hard she may balk and refuse to retrieve the others. There are a hundred and fifty of our people still trapped down there."

"You must convince her, Qaezul."

Turning around to face him, my temper flared. "I said I would speak to her."

Duke pinched his lips but kept silent. I ran my hand over my braid again. It didn't give me the comfort it once did. Since the change, the texture of my skin and hair no longer felt the same.

"Zaktaul is assessing the state of the garden," Duke said, breaking the uncomfortable silence between us.

Grateful for the change of topic, I perked up. After the Miners had exhausted the resources in the cave, a number of them had joined the Hunters and Gatherers to have a new purpose following the departure of the Creator. Although not as knowledgeable as the valos of that class, Zak could help get things moving again.

"The mirror system needs repairs after centuries of disuse. They are not realigning properly with the movement of the sun. The crops get too little light during the day. Once functional again, he'll be able to provide Lydia with more variety for her meals."

I caught myself almost shaking my head again at Duke's comment, but this time, in agreement. My Lydia had a healthy appetite and seemed open to trying new things. The way her ability constantly drained her, she would welcome diversity in what she ate to recharge.

"She will be most appreciative, I'm sure," I said with gratitude.

"The lower-city isn't adapted to Lydia's needs. She should stay here or I can clear another—"

"No," I interrupted, bristling at the suggestion. "She stays with m… us. We're not isolating her."

I averted my eyes and tweaked the waist of my loincloth that didn't need adjusting. Duke spared me the humiliation of pointing out my slip of the tongue.

"It should be her decision to make," he countered. I opened my mouth to argue but he didn't give me a chance to speak. "If *she* wishes to stay in the lower-city, I will build a hygiene room and a kitchen for her. Remember your own words, Qaezul; she's not our slave to be ordered about."

I lowered my head, dismayed by my irrational behavior. A sour taste filled my mouth.

What if she prefers to live alone in the upper-city?

Duke's heavy steps approached. Stopping in front of me, he raised a hand and rested it on my shoulder. A sympathetic expression softened the sharp lines of his high cheekbones and made his wide eyes appear a tad smaller.

Unfrozen

"Lydia is an intriguing female. She seems to have a good heart and looks at you with kind eyes. I do not begrudge you the emotions you feel. She has awakened your protective instincts. It is not my place to question or challenge it. Nature will follow its course however it sees fit."

Duke placed his second hand on my other shoulder, his glowing blue eyes, a shade darker than mine, leveled on me.

"However, remember well, my brother, that she is a stranger. You know nothing about her except that she too came from the sky."

That stung. I shrugged to pull out of his grasp but his hands tightened on my shoulders.

"The Strangers abandoned us without a word, leaving despair in their wake. Until we know why she's here, guard your heartstone well so she doesn't destroy you… and us."

"She won't."

"You don't know that, Qaezul."

"SHE WON'T!"

"She won't what?" Lydia's gentle voice called out behind me.

Duke's head jerked left to look at her and I spun around. My brain ceased to function. Lava burned in my chest, my heartstone glowing so bright it nearly blinded me.

So beautiful…

Although too big for her, the tunic flowed effortlessly down her slim body. The length of garment hid nothing of her long, slender legs, despite falling almost to her knees. The light blue fabric, a perfect match to the color of her almond-shaped eyes, made them pop. She'd somehow managed to tame her hair, tying it in a single long braid that dropped over her shoulder, down to her breasts.

I realized my feet had carried me over to her when my hand reached out to touch her braid. It caressed my palm as I slid my hand down its length. The rise and fall of her chest accelerated and the pulse on her neck picked up. My eyes locked with hers and my heartstone flared, its heat diffusing through my chest, down to my belly. Her pupils dilated and her lips parted.

"You look stunning," I whispered.

Lydia's gaze lowered to my lips. For some reason, my body responded with my rod stiffening. The fire in my belly made me ache.

Duke cleared his throat, ruining the moment. Lydia blinked and took a couple of step back, a guilty look settling on her face. The tips of her strange, rounded ears took on a reddish hue.

"Thank you," she said, fiddling with one of the overly long sleeve of her tunic.

It took me a second to understand what she was thanking me about.

"I hope you enjoyed your bath," Duke said, behind me.

I stepped back and turned sideways so that I could see both of them and gave him a warning glance. He ignored me.

"Yes, thank you, Duke."

She beamed at him and walked into the living area.

"And thank you for the fabulous clothes."

"My pleasure, Lydia."

Duke waved at the interior of the house.

"These dwellings have many accommodations which the lower-city lacks, since valos don't have the same needs you and the Strangers do."

I clasped my hands behind my back to hide their angry clenching and forced a neutral expression on my face.

"Yes, they are quite impressive," Lydia said, her voice hesitant.

Despite my efforts, she could sense something was off.

"Would you like to settle here or in one of the other mansions? I can clear the path for you," Duke offered.

Lydia cast a worried glance towards me.

"Is that what you were discussing when I arrived?" she asked.

"We discussed many topics," Duke answered non-committal. "Including that one, yes."

"Do you want me to stay here?" she asked, her gaze riveted on me.

"I want you to stay wherever you will feel the happiest," I said.

"Then I'd rather stay with you," she said without hesitation.

I couldn't hold back a grin and a triumphant look aimed at Duke. He snorted, his eyebrow twitching.

"Very well. I will build a hygiene room and kitchen for you in the lower-city then."

Lydia's hand flew to her chest, her eyes widening.

"Oh no! You don't need to do that!" she said, shaking her head.

Duke cast a furtive glance my way, a mocking smirk stretching his lips, having recognized the gesture I'd done earlier.

"I don't mind coming back up here when I need to use the facilities," Lydia added.

"It is no trouble, Lydia," Duke said. "Building is my purpose. It will take a few days to complete. In the meantime, let me show you how to operate the kitchen here when you want warm food."

"All right. Thank you."

Her eyes glimmered with gratitude as we watched him walk to the dais at the end of the living area. He climbed the three steps and indicated yet another hidden switch to open the invisible doors to the dining and kitchen area. I had never known if the Strangers hid everything out of secrecy or tidiness. From all accounts, they had behaved in a similar fashion in other cities.

Duke gave her a quick tour of the kitchen, showing her how to access and operate the grill, oven, and heated plates. He also indicated the location of the polished stone plates our Crafters had made and the metal utensils acquired through trade with the City of Light. Before taking his leave, he showed her the Strangers' bedrooms and wardrobes, telling her to put on the bed anything she wanted brought down for her.

With one last meaningful glance my way, Duke turned around and left. No sooner did he exit the bedroom than the weight of Lydia's stare settled on me.

"What's going on, Kai?" she asked, her voice filled with suspicion. "Why were you arguing about me?"

I sighed and indicated for her to follow me into the living area. Too many distracting thoughts coursed through my mind for us to stay in the privacy of the bedroom. Lydia sat on one of the long stone benches covered with a thick, red cushion. I settled next to her and turned my head to face her, wishing I could have pulled her on my lap again instead.

She studied my face as if she could find the answer in my features.

Choosing my words with care, I explained to her the source of our concern, stressing that while her welfare remained paramount, time flowed against us.

"Of course, I will help," Lydia said, sounding a little offended. "Letting your brothers die would be murder. Why would you even doubt my willingness to assist?"

"We did not doubt you, Lydia," I said with conviction. "But you collapsed in my arms this morning. I fear for your safety. The thought you might drop from exhaustion too far away for me to rescue you makes my heartstone ache."

Her eyelids fluttered and her blunt, white teeth grazed her lower lip. Reaching out to me, her delicate hand rested on top of mine in a comforting gesture, sending a pleasant jolt through me.

"I'm fine, Kai. I overextended myself this morning but now I know better."

She looked up and to the side, her face taking on a pensive expression.

"There were quite a few heartstones with weak or flickering lights." She refocused on me, grim determination settling on her features. "I need to retrieve them as soon as possible. If I pace myself and only use freeze when carrying the heartstones, I should be able to make two or three trips tonight."

My chest swelled with something beyond respect and gratitude. Pride came to mind. Lydia wasn't mine to be proud of, and yet a bond had taken root between us. A bond I intended to nurture until it blossomed.

"Thank you, Lydia."

Taking her hand between both of mine, I gave it a gentle squeeze and our eyes locked. In that instant, I wanted nothing more than to drown in the frozen depths of her eyes. Lydia's intoxicating presence made my heartstone throb and my mind splinter. Her lips brushing against mine confirmed I hadn't hallucinated her leaning forward. My abdominal muscles clenched, desire spreading its wings into the pit of my stomach. The contact of her mouth, soft and warm against mine, awakened a ravenous hunger deep within me. Releasing her hand, I raised mine to cup the back of her head, holding her in place. I pressed my lips harder against hers. She allowed it for a moment before pulling back. I fought the instinct to tighten my hold and let her go.

The delicate tip of her pink tongue licked her lips, then she smiled.

"I like you, Kai," she whispered. "You're a nice guy."

Head swimming, I latched onto the only coherent thought I felt capable of.

"Guy?" I asked.

She giggled, eyes crinkling. "Man, though you probably say male. You're a nice male."

"You're a nice female," I said, beaming at her.

My smile faded when her gaze dropped to my exposed teeth. Their sharpness had previously scared her. I didn't want her to ever fear me and especially, I didn't want her to touch her mouth to mine again. It made me feel wonderful things.

"Do not fear my teeth, Lydia. I promise to never eat you."

She laughed again. I loved the sound of her laugher, like the tinkling murmur of the water running down the river, flowing over me in a gentle caress.

"I don't fear your teeth. They're a part of you. I know you don't want to hurt me, so they won't either."

My throat constricted and my chest burned from the heat of my heartstone. She wasn't of my kind, but never had I felt such strong attraction to a female. Duke said nature would follow its course however it saw fit, but I intended to give it a nudge in a specific direction.

―――

EAGER TO GET STARTED on retrieving the heartstones, Lydia postponed searching the Stranger's bedroom and wardrobe to another time. She did take a moment to look at their footwear, only to pass on them as they were far too big for her small feet. During her rest cycle, I would try to retrofit a pair for her until my Artisan brothers, once awakened, could make her custom ones.

Zak and Duke stood by my side at the entrance of the lowest level, bearing witness to Lydia's efforts. Withstanding the ambient heat in her natural form, Lydia headed to the Miners' altar, the furthest one down the path. Only once there, her brown skin covered with frost, making it almost blend with the ice-blue fabric of her tunic.

Moving swiftly, she picked up a number of heartstones. I couldn't count how many from the distance. She placed them in a thin leather bag Duke had retrieved from one of the Strangers' dwellings. Without pausing, she raced back to the entrance, her arms wrapped around the pouch pressed to her chest. She released her frost as soon as she turned the curb into the last stretch towards us. Despite the heat, the chilled bag kept the heartstones cool.

Zak relieved her of the burden, deep respect shining in his eyes. Although it only contained eight heartstones, Lydia shook her arms and rolled her shoulders to shed the strain from them. This rescue demanded far more effort from her than any of us had realized. Zak turned on his heels and raced up the stairs to start seeking the owners of his precious package.

"How are you feeling?" I asked, my eyes flicking between hers.

She smiled. "I'm fine. Those things are heavy, though. I'll probably stick to five or six per trip instead. At least, I got all the weaker ones from the last altar. I'll have to use my frost on a shorter distance so I might be able to make more trips."

I didn't bother hiding the worry on my face. "Please be careful, Lydia."

"Don't worry, I will be."

She pressed her lips against mine. Before I could react, she pulled away and turned toward Duke who stared at us with bulging eyes. Lydia grabbed a second leather bag from his hand and headed back down the path. Duke's glowing gaze bore down on me. I gave him a sideway glance and shrugged my shoulders like Lydia often did to indicate she didn't know or it didn't matter.

"She likes me."

"You're becoming as strange as your female, Qaezul."

Unable to resist the urge, I shook my head up and down. He laughed and I turned my gaze back to *my* female.

Chapter 8

LYDIA

It took three more trips to retrieve the heartstones most at risk. I'd wanted to go out for another round but my arms felt like each had a block of concrete attached to them. My legs might as well have been made of cotton and balked at every step. There was no point overdoing it. Technically, I could wait a few days and the remaining heartstones would be fine.

Kai carried me all the way back to the upper-city, shielding me as best he could from the line of sight of his brothers. Their screams as they reunited with their soul—at least that's how I perceived it—were gut-wrenching. I didn't ask why he took me straight to the Stranger's mansion. With so many valos who had been on the verge of giving up, my presence held too great a risk of sending them over the edge like poor Seibkal.

When we entered the house, a large feast had been laid out on the coffee table in the living area. Scaled for the Strangers, the chairs of the dining table in the kitchen were too high and uncomfortable for me. Duke had come up to prepare it for me while I retrieved the other heartstones.

Kai sat me on the long bench with the red cushion and settled by my side. Despite his reluctance to leave me and as much as I wanted him nearby, I coaxed him to go back down and help his brothers. Twenty-three newly awakened valos, scared and disoriented would be too much for Zak and Duke to handle on their own. He sighed, then cast a hopeful look at my lips before locking eyes with me. I smiled, then kissed him.

His heartstone flared, its heat radiating against my chest. My nipples pebbled. As much as I wanted to indulge in the comfort of him, I pulled away and ran my thumb over his plump bottom lip. Kai's eyes glowed a darker shade of blue.

"I like when you press your mouth against mine," he said, his voice deeper than normal.

I chuckled. He was so damn cute.

"It's called a kiss. I like kissing you too."

"A kiss…" he repeated, lengthening the *s* almost into a hiss. "You can kiss me anytime you want. As often as you want."

I laughed again and his eyebrows did that adorable twitchy thing.

"You might regret saying that when I start doing it too often," I said, teasingly.

He shook his head with such energy I feared it might fly off his neck.

"Never too often. You can do whatever you want to me, whenever you want. I like your strange ways."

A ball of fire exploded in the pit of my stomach and my skin heated. There were many things I would want to do to him.

"Okay," I breathed out, holding the hem of my tunic in tight fists.

"I must tend to my brothers now. I will return when they are settled," Kai said, rising to his feet. "Eat, my Lydia. You need to regain your strength."

My Lydia.

The possessiveness of it... the way in which he'd just claimed me made me feel all warm and fuzzy.

Legs closed, I tried to ignore the dull throbbing below as he walked away. Kai's body was perfection; tall and lean, just on the right side of muscular without entering beefy territory. And his behind... That loincloth didn't hide the nicely rounded bump underneath. I wanted to explore every parcel of his body, especially to confirm to what extent we were compatible. Ice Valo he might be, but a fire lay dormant beneath his cool exterior.

A wave of weariness washed over me when Kai exited the house. I turned to the aromatic food sprawled before me. To my surprise, the fish steaks had already been seared and sat on a heated plate. I hoped Duke hadn't suffered too much discomfort preparing them. I chowed down the six pieces, barely chewing in between each bite. Next, I picked up what resembled an energy bar. Although I could see the gurahn berries inside, it tasted more savory than sweet. The roasted cereals and nuts crunched beneath my teeth. If a little dry, it was another nice addition to the menu.

I poured some of the pink juice from a glass jar into a giant cup. Too big to wrap my fingers around it, I held the glass with both hands like a baby bottle and gulped down its content. It tasted like pink lemonade with a touch of candied apple. I got halfway through one half of a plain riverfruit before my belly begged for mercy.

My eyes drooped. A glance at the bedroom door showed it to be close yet too damn far away. If I forced myself

Unfrozen

up, I would get there in ten seconds. But staying right here, I could nap on this bench and would hear Kai when he returned. The bed would be far more comfortable but I also might oversleep. After five minutes of mental tug-of-war, I wanted to kick myself. Had I just gotten off my lazy ass the instant the urge to sleep overcame me, I'd be curled up in bed now instead of nodding off.

Fuck it, I'll just nap here.

I laid down on the plush cushion of the bench. It was long enough for me to stretch my whole length and wide enough that I probably wouldn't roll off. A contented sigh escaped my throat as sleep claimed me.

A volcano erupted inside me, setting my blood on fire and burning my skin to a crisp. I couldn't breathe. Each air intake fanned the fire setting me ablaze. My brain boiled, trapped in the confines of my skull. I struggled against the restraints that strapped me down.

Why were they doing this to me? Why me?

A frantic voice spoke incomprehensible words to my dying brain. Dr. Sobin, I assumed. If I didn't cool down, I'd combust. Gathering what will I had left, I lowered my temperature as far as I could. Rather than the relief I had hoped for, liquid fire poured over me.

I screamed.

My body shook with violent tremors, no doubt the spasms of death throes. I would welcome it. Anything but this never-ending torture.

"Let me die. Please, let me die."

"NO!" Kai's voice yelled.

My eyes snapped open. Emerging from the horrendous dream, I found myself tangled in a burning furnace.

"Get it off!! GET IT OFF!" I shouted, struggling to remove the heavy, red comforter that pinned me to the massive bed.

With one fluid movement, Kai tore it off me and tossed it across the room. It thumped against the wall and crumpled to the floor in a ripple of fabric. Cool air slapped my burning skin and I threw myself into Kai's arms, sobbing. He hissed, his body stiffening at the contact, but he didn't push me away.

"My Lydia," he whispered, holding me tight. "You cannot die. I won't let you die."

A sheet of ice formed around him, further cooling me down. I welcomed it and pressed myself harder against him.

"I was burning alive."

Tears choked me. I'd been back on that dreaded operating table, at the mercy of that heartless monster who dared call herself a scientist.

"I'm so sorry, my Lydia," Kai said, his voice broken with shame. "I never meant to hurt you."

I lifted my face to look at him through my tears. Sorrow contorted his features.

"It's not your fault. I had a nightmare," I said between sniffles.

Kai shook his head and sat at the edge of the bed, cradling me on his lap.

"You fell asleep on the bench. I brought you here to make you more comfortable. You shivered a few times so I put that blanket on you," he said, pointing at the blanket on the floor. "The Strangers always used them."

Unfrozen

I frowned at the white blanket on the floor. Despite my shock, I could have sworn it had been a different color when I woke.

"I thought it was red…" I whispered, confused.

"It was," Kai confirmed, guilt burning in his eyes. "As soon as I put it on you, it changed color. Duke said the blanket adjusts to maintain your body temperature at the appropriate level. You were fine at first but then you started tossing and turning. Then the blanket turned a darker shade of red. At first, I thought it was the problem so I almost removed it but then you started talking in your sleep. You were begging someone to stop, asking why they were doing this to you. Who has hurt you, my Lydia?"

Of course, that made sense. The blanket would have been regulated to the Strangers' temperature. Considering their greater height, they probably also had a higher body temperature than mine. If the blanket tried to regulate my temperature to what it considered standard, I would have lowered mine to maintain what my own body knew to be right. The blanket would have heated further to compensate, then on and on in a vicious cycle until it was all but cooking me once I went into my lowest frost level.

I shuddered, wondering how far things could have gone had Kai not awakened me.

His arms tightened around me. "You are safe. I won't let anyone harm you."

"I know." I snuggled against him and rested my head on his shoulder. "Some very bad people hurt me, experimented on me to change me."

Kai's hard body stiffened. "The Creators got you too?"

The odd softness of his skin rubbed against my cheek as I shook my head.

"No, not the Creators. Other humans like me."

"*Yoomanz?*" Kai asked.

"My species. You are valo, I am human."

"I understand. Why would your own people hurt you?"

I lifted my head to look at him, his dusty blue skin looking almost white in the dimmed light of the bedroom.

"Humans aren't bad, but some people can become very cruel and heartless when driven by greed or the thirst for power. And when that happens, they will hurt anyone, even innocents to achieve their goals."

"Before the change, we sometimes had dysfunctional people that couldn't or wouldn't be redeemed. They would be banned from the tribes to seek the mercy of Sonhadra."

"Humans have something similar but we don't ban people, we put them in prison. Depending on the severity of the crime, the person can be kept there for a short time or the rest of their life. They put me in a prison like that, out in space, where I was to stay until I died."

"What is a prison?"

I pursed my lips, pondering.

"Do you know what a cage is?" I asked.

"A trap with bars the Hunters use to catch predators or prey."

I smiled. "Yes, exactly. A prison is a dwelling with many cages where you put people to punish them."

Kai recoiled and pulled back to look down at my face, the glowing of his eyes casting a shadow on the sharp edges of his cheekbones.

"That is very cruel! They would have put you in a cage for the rest of your life? Why?"

While I didn't relish causing him distress, Kai's dismay and agitation made me all fuzzy inside. I loved that he cared enough about my welfare to show outrage on my behalf. It felt good to be wanted and protected, especially by someone as sweet as my valo.

"Back on Earth, my home world, I used to work for a pharmaceutical company. We created medicine to heal people—or at least that was the mandate. The scientists there made all kinds of experiments to discover the cures for serious diseases. Sometimes those experiments went wrong and tragedy occurred. A little over a year ago, such an accident happened and a virus leaked out, killing almost everyone in my small town."

My stomach coiled remembering the incident that had destroyed my life and set it on this most improbable course.

"But it didn't kill you. Were you away?"

"No, I was right there in the middle of it all. Everyone became very sick, very quickly. Most people died within two or three days. The others lingered for a week. They had quarantined our town. Blocked external access to the city and prevented people from leaving to contain the epidemic," I specified when Kai gave me a confused look. "Everyone died except those who had made it to the shelters in time, and me. But I hadn't made it to the shelters. My body refused to let the virus win. According to the medical report, my vital functions dropped very low, like my body hibernated while dealing with the threat. Then my temperature would rise to abnormally high levels that should have killed me but killed the virus instead, little by little. It took three weeks but my body eventually won the fight and I woke up, weak but cured."

"My Lydia is strong," Kai said, his voice dripping with pride.

Loving the possessive way in which he claimed me, my lips stretched with contentment. I snuggled deeper against him and traced the outline of his heartstone with my fingertips. Its glow brightened and it warmed beneath my touch.

"Most of my family had been out of town, so thankfully they were spared. After waking up, I wanted to go to them and mourn the terrible losses before deciding what to do next with my life. Instead, I was thrown in jail and accused of being part of a group of rebels and radicals that deliberately caused the tragedy."

Kai's cool palm caressed my hand in a comforting gesture, tempering the anger creeping in my voice.

"Why did they falsely accuse you?"

"Because they needed someone to blame and they wanted me at their mercy. I shouldn't have survived the epidemic. Something in my genetics made me different and they wanted full access to it. The pharmaceutical company I worked for was part of a larger group of companies, including The Orchid Company which specialized in finding people with unique genetic traits, like me and making them disappear."

I shifted on Kai's lap. His hand slid down to my bare thigh, resting just above my knee. My skin tingled.

"The trial was a farce. They fabricated enough evidence against me to have me sentenced to life with no chance of pardon. As soon as I reached the *Concord*, a space prison where all the worst criminals are kept, I lost all my rights and privileges as a human being."

I explained the horror of life aboard the ship and how a wormhole—probably—pulled the ship into Sonhadra's gravitational pull and crash-landed us here. He got so upset, I had to pause a few times to soothe him. When I told him about the creatures that hunted me and how mushroom poisoning almost caused me to drown, he freaked out.

"We have mushrooms here too, but not the purple ones," Kai said, still agitated. "I have never heard of any mushroom making people sick, even those you ate. You will not eat any of them here without doing a small sample test first. In fact, we will not give you new food without a test to make sure it will not hurt you."

I bristled at the finality of his tone and almost argued. Although my gluttonous nature rebelled at the thought, his concerns remained valid. The way I'd been overtaxing myself the past few days, another food poisoning crisis might do me in. Unlike Quinn, my scientist hadn't engineered me to be immortal. I wouldn't survive a high enough dose of poison or a slit to the throat.

"Fine," I mumbled.

Kai chuckled and lifted his hand from my thigh to pinch my pouting lip. That made me smile. Everything about him made me smile. Well… maybe not those crazy shark teeth of his but even they were growing on me. A future on Sonhadra didn't sound so terrible anymore. But would the other valos come to accept me like Kai did?

"How are your brothers?"

"They are well. We suffered no casualty this time."

Air rushed out of me and a weight I didn't realize I carried lifted a bit from my shoulders. The vision of Seibkal smashing his heartstone still haunted me.

"They are a bit confused but grateful for you." He caressed my hair, his hand coming to a stop on my cheek. "As am I."

I turned my face to kiss his palm then looked back at him. His eyes were locked on my lips. Leaning forward, I rubbed my nose against the tiny bump of his before kissing his lips. A groan rumbled through his chest when I sucked on his thicker bottom lip. I gave it a little nip before letting go. His tongue, a paler shade of ice blue, peeked out to lick his lip.

"I really like this kissing thing," he grumbled.

I burst out laughing and opened my mouth to answer but nearly dislocated my jaw instead with a sudden yawn. Kai stared at me with bulging eyes, mouth gaping. No wonder, considering I'd given him an up-close view of my tonsils before I managed to put my hand in front of my mouth. My ears and cheeks heated.

"Sorry," I said, scrunching my face. "It happens sometimes to humans as a sign we're tired. We have no control over it."

Kai blinked then his eyebrows did their little dance again.

"Are you mocking me?" I asked in false outrage.

"Maybe," he said, smiling. "Humans are strange."

"You have no idea," I mumbled.

"Sleep, my Lydia. I will keep watch."

He rose to his feet, still holding me cradled to his chest, then turned around to lay me down on the bed. I snatched his hand as he straightened.

"Won't you get bored?" I asked.

"No, I won't."

I bit my lip, not wanting to come on too strong.

Fuck it. Worse case he'll say no.

"If you're going to keep watch, would you lie down next to me?"

His heartstone flared and his mouth opened and closed a few times before he blurted out, "I would like that very much."

I grinned and scooted over to the side to make room for him. Despite his size, the bed was humongous, large enough to accommodate four valos comfortably. Kai lay down on his back. Sneaking an arm around his waist, I buried my face in the crook of his neck. His own arm wrapped around my back, holding me to him.

"Sleep well, my Lydia," Kai said. "I will keep you safe."

I kissed his neck and closed my eyes, smiling at the purring rumble of his chest.

THE FOLLOWING MORNING, Kai forced me to stop my rescue efforts after the second trip. I was tiring too quickly and the urgency had passed. The remaining heartstones glowed strong enough that I could pace myself. We agreed I would perform two rounds every morning, for a total of twelve new valos awakened a day. At this rate, it would take six more days to retrieve all the heartstones from the altars along the main path. The huge cluster on the central island remained the issue.

Both the lower and upper-city boomed with activity. The valos remained nervous in my presence, especially the Hunter class. When I asked Kai why, he explained that the Tarakheen trampled their moral and spiritual beliefs. Although omnivore, their tribes held a great respect for life. You didn't hunt for pleasure or frivolous purposes. You shouldn't kill a nursing mother just because her fur had a unique color and was the softest right after birthing. You didn't hunt a species to the verge of extinction only to harvest a tiny gland from their corpse to use in a lab and discard the rest.

The tribes only took a life to protect and provide. They used and consumed everything from their kills all the way down to making tools and utensils from the teeth and bones. The Hunters had been among the first to sow the seed of rebellion. With their heartstones returned, the memory of all they had done under the Creator's compulsion came crashing down on them. It was a tremendous amount of guilt to work through, even though it hadn't been of their free will. They didn't trust yet another stranger from the sky that looked a little too much like a Creator even though they knew I wasn't one.

Therefore, aside from my rescue missions, I made myself scarce in the lower-city. It sucked feeling isolated, but Kai went out of his way to keep me entertained and gave me a tour of the upper-city. That Creator and her Strangers had a thing for hidden switches and rooms. We made it a game to try and discover as many of them on our own without spoilers from Duke.

This morning, as I completed my second trip, with less than two dozen heartstones remaining along the outer walls, it dawned on me that I didn't know who those located on the island belonged to. Most of the alcoves now stood empty. There were far more heartstones left than sleeping valos. Where were the others?

After handing over the second bag to Duke, I asked Kai about it. He looked troubled for a moment then seemed to make a decision. Taking my hand, he led me up the stairs, then made an ice platform to bring us to the Builders level on the second floor. Under the distrustful stares of his brothers, we marched toward the back. My stomach knotted as we approached a door—the first I had seen in the lower-city—made of thick, opaque ice. Kai touched a hand to the frozen surface and it peeled away, folding over the white stone door frame like a glossy curtain.

My breath caught in my throat.

Knees shaking, I stepped into the circular room. Although identical in shape and size as the greeting hall on the top floor, this one felt claustrophobic. Sunlight, reflected by the mirror system warmed my skin while the frosty air trickling in through the vents pierced in the ornate walls chilled me to the bone.

Approximately forty alcoves lined the entire length of the wall. Within them, female valos stared into the distance, trapped in their eternal slumber. A dozen more alcoves, divided in two groups of six, framed a stone altar in the middle. Behind the altar, a single alcove stood watching over it.

With a will of their own, my legs carried me to the altar, bile rising in my throat. My hand flew to my mouth, holding in my pained cry.

Not an altar.

I swallowed the bitter taste in my mouth as I gazed into the cradle. Tiny hands half fisted on each side of an infant's small body. His bare feet tucked inwards as he lay on his back, empty, ice-blue eyes staring at the ceiling. His small, bony chest pulsated with a flickering heartstone covered with a translucent layer of skin.

Tears welled in my eyes. Clinging to the edge of the stone cradle for support, I turned my disbelieving gaze toward Kai.

"Babies? The Creator has done this to babies too?"

Kai tore his eyes away from the child and stared back at me. Shoulders tense, a nerve ticked at his temple. At the edge of my vision, I noted the group of valos that had gathered behind him. They watched me closely, broadcasting loud waves of wariness and aggression. I was too distraught to feel scared of them.

"The Creator did not make the child. He was born after the change," Kai said, his voice filled with hatred.

He walked up to the cradle and caressed the baby's bald head.

"His arrival was the final trigger that caused Tarakheen to take away our heartstones."

My teeth clenched. What the hell kind of bitch would harm a child?

"But he has his heartstone," I argued, looking at the naked form of the child. "Why does he hibernate?"

"We are unsure. He became unresponsive the day Tarakheen removed his mother's heartstone. He was the first to enter this state." Kai lifted his head to look at the sole female overlooking the cradle. "This is his mother, Riaxan'dak Var O'Tuk. She was a great Hunter before her pregnancy, and an amazing Gatherer. No one could catch liexor like she did. It's a type of shellfish," he specified at my questioning look.

Kai walked up to Riaxan and adjusted the multi-row necklace of gems and beads that hung down, over her small, naked breasts.

"In the days before she gave birth, when her breasts swelled for nursing, the scent of fish started to make her nauseous, so she stopped fishing for them."

That comment gave me pause. Looking around the room at the other females, I realized to my shock that they were all flat-chested like the males. But their bone structure, more refined facial features, and curvier bodies screamed female—at least by human standards.

"Two other Gatherers took over the task but were nowhere near as successful. Tarakheen was greedy when it came to eating liexor. When we repeatedly failed to supply the demand, she sent some of the Strangers to investigate."

I hugged my mid-section, sensing where this was headed.

"We had kept the baby's existence a secret. It had been easy since the Strangers never came here and didn't pay us much attention. It was beneath them. But with the wind of rebellion already stirring among the Hunters, Tarakheen's people were more vigilant. They heard the cries of the baby and reported back to her."

Kai ran a hand over his braid, a tortured look on his face as he recounted the events. A few of the other males muttered under their breaths, anger etched on their faces.

"She demanded to see the baby. When we refused, the Strangers used the devices on their wrists to control us. The pain was terrible, like clawed hands crushing our heartstones and tearing our very souls from our bodies."

Kai's hand covered his heartstone as if he could still feel the pain.

"Tarakheen was furious. She screamed at Riaxan for disrespecting her by giving life. This city only had one mother: her. None other would birth offspring until she birthed her own. She became even angrier when she realized the baby's heartstone couldn't be removed or controlled. In her rage, she tore out Riaxan's heartstone and ordered her people to remove them from every female."

"She took away my mate, my child, and all of our females out of spite!" spat a big, burly valo standing among those observing us. "And then she took away our minds so we couldn't fight back."

His hands, fisted by his sides, trembled with barely repressed rage. But it was the pain and the longing twisting his features that tore at my heart. Tears welled in my eyes again at the selfish cruelty of that woman.

"This is so wrong… We have to get them out, Kai." My voice shook with emotion. "I need a way onto the island."

He walked up to me and cupped my face in his cold hands. "We are looking for one and we will find it."

Kai pulled me into his embrace and I hugged him back, my heart breaking at the thought of that tiny body trapped in an endless sleep before his life had even started.

Turning my head to the side, I made eye contact with Riaxan's mate.

"I will get her back. This, I promise you. I will get them all back."

Chapter 9

KAI

My fingers combed through Lydia's tight black curls. I marveled once again at the soft, bouncy texture. It had taken much coaxing to convince her to leave them unbound at night so I could play with them. She said it got too huge and puffy, like a giant black sun around her head when not controlled in a neat braid.

Nonsense.

My Lydia was beautiful, especially with her unruly mane.

I tightened my hold around her, purring with contentment. Spending my nights with Lydia's warm body wrapped around mine proved to be the most pleasurable torment. For the past four days, it had become our new ritual. I could no longer imagine spending an entire day without those special hours with just the two of us. Her breath fanned my chest, my heartstone matched its pulse to her heartbeat, and her skin caressed mine with each of her movements.

Lydia moved a lot.

She didn't toss and turn but fidgeted, rubbing her face against my neck, running her hand up and down my chest, and wrapping her leg around mine. Sometimes, I thought she was trying to climb on top of me.

I loved it.

Other times, like now, her tunic would ride up and expose the curve of her behind. It ignited my fire and made my rod harden. I knew she didn't have a rod too because she often rubbed against me and I felt nothing between her legs. Well, moisture once and the intoxicating scent of her musk during one agitated night. Lydia's dream had been intense. She had been restless and said my name a few times. My imagination had run wild as to what she might have dreamt about. I hadn't dared to ask her in the morning.

Lydia stirred, her hand sliding down my shoulder to cup my heartstone. She inhaled deeply before heaving a sigh. My pulse picked up with anticipation; she was awakening. Pressing herself against me, Lydia turned her head and kissed my chest. That did nothing to lessen my arousal. I debated whether to get out of bed to hide my condition or stay put. Where nudity and sexuality were concerned, I didn't quite know where she stood.

I still remembered her embarrassment at undressing before us that first time we showed her the bath. Yet, she had no problems making physical contact with me, touching and kissing me. In fact, she appeared to relish it and seized every opportunity to do so. That pleased me. I wanted to do more with her but feared she might take offense.

Nudity and sexuality were natural to my people. As long as the joining occurred between people of sufficient maturity and both freely gave their consent, then all was well. Any offspring resulting from it would be welcomed as a cause for rejoicing within the tribe, whether the couple decided to become life mates or not. Imagining Lydia's belly swollen with my offspring set my heartstone ablaze.

"Someone's flaring up," Lydia whispered against my chest. "What were you thinking about?"

Her fingertips drew little circles on my heartstone. She kissed my nipple then lifted her head to look at me.

"You," I said.

She raised an eyebrow. "Oh? What about me?"

Her fingers strayed to my other nipple and resumed their circular motion around it. I gnashed my teeth, swallowing the moan rising in my throat.

"Y… Your tunic… rode up in your sleep."

She cast a glance at her exposed rear then looked back at me, her pale blue eyes darkening.

"Does it bother you?"

Her voice dropped into a husky whisper. My rod throbbed in response. I didn't quite know how to respond. She frowned when I delayed to answer.

"Nudity doesn't bother me or my people. It is natural."

"But?" she persisted.

"Yours makes me feel things," I said, eyeing her warily.

"Good things, I hope?"

Her naked leg moved up over mine, her thigh brushing against my sack.

"Yes," I said in a strangled voice. "But I know it offends your people."

She chuckled and shook her head. "Nudity doesn't offend my people. We just don't like showing ourselves naked in public. But I don't mind being naked in front of you."

My abdominal muscles contracted as her palm slid down my stomach to rest right below my navel.

"Only you," she whispered before stretching her neck to kiss my lips.

Unable to resist any further, I slipped my hand down her back to grab the bare flesh of her rounded backside.

So soft and warm...

Lydia climbed on top of me, her breasts brushing against my chest. The weight and warmth of her wrapped around me, scalding my insides with desire. She slipped her hands behind my head and nipped my bottom lip before sucking it into her mouth. I loved when she did that, or anything else that involved her touching me.

"Someone is happy to see me," she said, her breath caressing my lips.

Hips moving from side to side, she rubbed her groin on my erection. Heat spread further and a groan of pleasure rumbled in my chest. Grabbing her other bottom cheek with my left hand, I pressed her against me, hiding nothing of my desire.

Lydia broke the kiss, her mouth trailing along my jawline to my ear. The warm wetness of her tongue traced its outline, fueling the fire within. I slipped one hand beneath her tunic, up the arched curve of her back. Searing heat met my palm. She was my sun; giving me life, lighting my heartstone, and melting the ice in my veins.

She shivered, her skin erupting in those strange little bumps from the coolness of my touch. They tickled my palms as I ran my hands over the intriguing phenomenon. Pushing up and away from me, Lydia sat on her haunches, our sexes aligned. Eyes locked with mine, she grabbed the hem of the yellow tunic she had worn to bed last night, pulled it up and over her head. With a flick of her wrist, she tossed it to the floor. My gaze roamed over her, mesmerized by the warm brown color of her skin and the darker circle around her generous breasts. I had never seen any this big. Round and perky, their hard buds pointed at me, taunting me.

As if reading my mind, Lydia grabbed my hands resting on her hips and brought them to her chest. I closed them around the perfect orbs. A soft moan slipped between Lydia's plump lips. She trembled and leaned into my touch. After finding out about our females, she had told me human females' breasts didn't flatten between pregnancies. Although relieved to know she had no infant longing for her in her home world, I still found it strange. Now though, I appreciated this quirk of my female.

Sitting up, I arched her backwards and covered her neck and chest with kisses. I rubbed my face against her skin, inhaling her fresh, crisp scent. Answering the call of her taunting nubs, I sucked one of her nipples into my mouth. Careful not to hurt her, I nipped at them before soothing them with my tongue. The salty sweetness of her skin made me hunger for more.

She shivered again and whispered my name.

I flipped us around so that she lay on her back. Her chest heaved faster, in tandem with her breathing. My hand caressed its way down her body to the small patch of hair between her legs. The mystery of what hid there had fueled my imagination for countless hours as she slept against me, or when I waited outside while she bathed. The thought that we might not be compatible knotted my insides.

Crawling backwards, I parted her legs and settled between them. She watched me with hooded eyes, her lips parted. The luscious scent of her musk tickled my nose, making my rod jerk beneath my loincloth. My fingertips twirled around the soft curls and Lydia's stomach quivered. Sliding my hand lower, I was surprised by the little nub that greeted me. I ran my thumb over it and Lydia shuddered, her moan resonating in my ears. Intrigued, I rubbed it faster, harder. More throaty moans answered my actions. Legs shaking, she fisted the blanket covering the bed.

Lydia's essence leaked from the opening between her dark, purple folds. Without stopping my ministrations to her nub, I slipped two fingers inside her, relieved to find her similar there to our females. Her channel contracted around my fingers. Though tight, she should be able to accept me without too much difficulty. My stomach tightened with the burning urge to bury myself inside her. I wrapped my hand at the base of my rod, squeezing it tightly to silence it.

Lydia's head tossed left and right on the pillow, her soft curls damp with sweat. Her blunt teeth bit into her bottom lip. I would see her reach completion first. More essence leaked out of her. Unable to resist, I pulled my fingers out and replace them with my mouth. Her back arched.

"Kai!" she screamed, her voice strangled.

The taste of her made my head spin. Tart and somewhat salty, I couldn't get enough. When I wrapped my lips around her nub and sucked on it, Lydia's hand closed in a tight grip around the braid at the back of my head, pressing my face to her core. I didn't need words to understand what she needed. I didn't stop until her body seized, then collapsed, shaking with the spasms of bliss.

Unfrozen

She looked so beautiful in her state of abandon, brown skin glistening like polished velax stones. Kneeling, I removed my loincloth. The feel of the fabric brushing against my skin almost abrasive in my need. Lydia half-dazed gaze ran over me, locking onto my rod. The way she licked her lips then smiled, it must have looked familiar in its form. She spread her legs wider and opened her arms invitingly.

My female...

A tender emotion tugged at me. My heartstone burned my chest, the heat spreading through my limbs in a wave of pleasure-pain. I crawled back up, laying down over her. I hissed at the contact of her burning skin. It hurt and yet felt so good seeping into me. Lydia wrapped her arms around me, and I sucked air in through my teeth at the searing touch. Her eyes widened, understanding the cause and she lowered her temperature.

"Don't!" I whispered against her lips. "I want you as you are."

She frowned, a concerned look on her face. "I don't want to hurt you."

I smiled. "Do not worry. I want your heat. I want your flame. I want all of you."

I pushed myself inside her. The wet inferno of her tight channel engulfed me. With slow thrusts at first, I began moving in and out of her. Each stroke threatened to set me on fire while her palms painted a blazing trail up and down my back. I held the sun in my arms and never wanted to let go. What did it matter if she burned me to cinders? I lost myself in her flame, her raspy moans filling my ears, an almost unbearable pleasure consuming me. In this instant, she was mine and I was hers.

The scream of her release and the convulsing hold of her channel sent me over the edge. I rocked in and out of her while my seed flowed into her in blissful spurts, cooling the furnace that gripped me.

Rolling onto my back, I pulled her over me. Lydia's racing heart pounded against my chest, her hot, labored breath blowing on my neck. I held her close, watching the plumes of steam rising from her skin where we touched.

My sun... My iwaki... My mate...

In that instant, something changed. I didn't know what, but I felt it in my heartstone.

LYDIA RETRIEVED TWELVE more heartstones over her two trips of the day. Tomorrow, the last of my brothers would be rescued, leaving the females still stranded out of reach. After awakening today's group and giving them a chance to get their bearings, we gathered in the main hall to address this issue. Over the past week, we'd held many discussions on how to get Lydia onto the island and back, unharmed.

The heat prevented us from getting close enough to build a proper bridge, and Lydia didn't have the strength required to carry slabs of stone. Even if we combined our efforts, an ice bridge wouldn't last—we tried—and the amount of steam created by the ice melting over the lava would seriously harm Lydia, not to mention the heartstones.

After much deliberation, we agreed to stack as many stone slabs as possible in one location and hope the lava lake wasn't too deep. It would be tricky. Truth be told, we didn't hold much hope it would work but with no other options, we had to at least give this a try. With everyone in agreement, we headed out to the quarry. On foot, it represented a long journey, but not for the Northern Valos.

I couldn't wait to take Lydia sliding.

As we marched toward the exit, my heartstone thrummed with emotion to be surrounded by my brothers. Eighty-three of us, strong, whole, and once more driven by both purpose and hope, thanks to the beautiful female by my side.

My female.

She smiled up at me and my hand tightened around hers.

Although they hadn't fully lowered their guard, my brothers were easing around her. They could sense the shift in my relationship with Lydia and didn't know how to handle it. In all fairness, I didn't quite know where we stood either. She liked me enough to wish to join with me, but was that all? Had she chosen me because I was the first to have interacted with her? Would she tire of me and turn to another?

I didn't want to entertain these thoughts. They made my heartstone burn in a most unpleasant way.

We climbed the stairs to the surface and lined up in the open plain sprawling before the city. Lydia gave me an expectant look, wondering what would happen. I grinned, no longer worried to show my sharp teeth since she had taught me to kiss with our tongues. This was another of her strange human ways I really enjoyed.

I planted my feet firmly on the ground, left foot forward, right foot facing to the side. Keeping a gap between them for greater balance, I summoned the frost and built an ice board beneath my feet, wide and thick enough for Lydia to ride with me. Her eyes widened and she cast furtive glances at the others who had also made smaller versions of the ice board beneath their own feet. Pulling her onto my board, I wrapped one arm around her waist and held her against me.

"Hold on tight," I said against her lips before planting a soft kiss on her mouth.

She embraced me, pressing her chest to my heartstone. For a moment, I wondered if the boots Zak had crafted for her out of the Strangers' old footwear might be too slippery for the ice board. As a precaution, I weaved a thin sheet of ice around her feet, strong enough to keep her from slipping but flimsy enough to break if she fell so she didn't harm her ankles.

Lydia squealed in surprise, her grip tightening around me when I pushed a blast of frost against the moisture in the air, propelling us forward. With each blast, our speed increased, the board sliding over the mostly even surface of the frozen plain. Soon, the crisp wind whipped around us. Lydia's laughter rang clear in my ears.

"This is awesome!" she shouted, between bouts of laughter. "Faster! Go faster!"

Pride and happiness filled my heartstone as I complied. A thin layer of frost coated her skin, making her as white as the packed snow covering the ground. I'd seen her like this before but never felt her body against mine in that state. As much as I loved the burn of her heat, this left me speechless. The cold gave her skin a slightly harder edge, making her feel like a valo. Would she be cold inside as well?

My rod stiffened at the thought. I almost wished I had allowed her to do it this morning when she'd wanted to. But I couldn't regret what we had shared and the searing warmth of her. There would be other times... I hoped.

"Let's pass him!" Lydia yelled, pointing at Neixor slightly ahead of us.

With only their own weight to carry, the others were ahead, some by a notable distance. Eager to please my female, I picked up the speed. Within seconds, we caught up then passed him. Lydia squealed in victory and pointed at the next target. By the fourth valo we passed, I was all in, enjoying the game. The others caught on in no time and fought back, competing against us and each other. By the time we reached the quarry, we were all laughing and in high spirits. It had been too long since we'd been this carefree.

Another gift from my female.

I released her feet from the sheet of ice and unraveled the ice board. Although far from E'Lek, this section of the cliff ran deep and wide. Gathering stones from it wouldn't threaten the stability of the ground beyond and the countless lifeforms that dwelled on the plateau.

I caressed Lydia's back through the red tunic she wore today, having declined the warmer coats the Strangers wore when travelling around the land. Eyes sparkling with excitement, she watched my brothers head toward the stone cliff. Their bodies swelled, grew taller and bulkier as they brought forth their battle form.

"Do not be afraid, my Lydia."

She wasn't.

Plump lips parted in awe, her gaze flicked this way and that, taking on the hulking forms of my brothers.

"*Bahdass...*" she whispered.

I didn't know the meaning of that word, but from her tone, I guessed it expressed admiration. She turned her luminous eyes towards me, an expectant look on her face. A sudden bout of shyness knotted my stomach. I ran my hand over my braid, feeling silly. Lydia had seen my battle form before, although under tragic circumstances. What if she didn't like it or found it ugly? What if it scared her again?

Her body may be fragile but my Lydia is strong.

She truly was strong, smart, and brave. A weak person couldn't have survived all she'd gone through since her people's betrayal and then crashing on Sonhadra.

Taking a couple of steps back, I summoned my battle form. The elastic band of my loincloth stretched to accommodate my broadening waist. Lydia appeared to shrink in size as I grew by two more heads above her. She had to throw her head all the way back to look up at me. The popping, crackling sound of ice expanding and reshaping me stopped with the last ice plate settling on my shoulder.

I stood still, my heartstone throbbing while awaiting her reaction. Without fear, Lydia stepped forward and raised her small palms to my chest. Having shed her frost, I looked in fascination at her beautiful dark skin roaming over my pale-blue plating. I wished my battle armor didn't block the warmth and softness of her touch. It only allowed me to perceive where her hands made contact and with how much strength, but no more.

Reaching up, she cradled my face in her hands and rose to the tip of her toes. I bent down and she pressed her lips to mine. My heartstone flared beneath the thick layer of ice shielding it. Careful not to wound her with the icy spikes on my arms and shoulders, I drew her into my embrace, and returned her kiss.

"My Lydia," I whispered, when she pulled back.

"My Kai," she replied, a tender look in her eyes.

A ball of fire exploded in my chest, spreading that pleasant heat through my limbs, all the way to the bone. I beamed at her for claiming me.

She started, her eyes bulging with shock.

"You better *not* eat me with those!"

I burst out laughing, and the bright peals of hers joined mine. In this form, everything was bigger, scarier. I could only imagine what my pointed teeth looked like to her considering I could sever the spine of creatures three times her size with them.

"Fear not, my Lydia. I care about you too much to eat you."

Despite their efforts to hide it, my brothers stole confused glances at us. I couldn't blame them. In their place, I too would have wondered why a valo would put his mouth against another person like that.

I built a wide block of ice for Lydia to sit on if she tired and, with much reluctance, left her to go aid my brothers. As Northern Valos, we all possessed a great affinity with water. We could sense it, even as mere moisture in the air, manipulate it and control its temperature. Using that, cutting off blocks of stone didn't require strength, but finesse and precision.

I stood in front of the rocky face of the quarry, next to the crease where I would dig. Pushing moisture into it, I froze just the amount required until the swelling ice fractured the stone. I unraveled the ice and repeated the process, cutting deeper into the crease to carve out a block of appropriate dimensions.

While working, I kept an eye on Lydia, not only to make sure no harm came to her, but because I couldn't resist the urge to gaze upon her. Such strange creatures, these humans.

She'd stacked three balls of snow, one atop another. The bottom was the biggest, with the top one being the smallest. Using stone chips found on the ground, she made what I assumed were eyes, a nose and a mouth on the small ball. I didn't understand the meaning of the eyes she made in a straight line on the middle ball. For a while afterward, she searched around the quarry, looking for something. When I asked her, she inquired if there were any dead trees nearby. She needed two branches for Frosty's arms. Apparently, that snow pile was male and famous among humans. I made her two thin branches of ice which she happily stuck to the sides of the middle ball to serve as arms for Frosty.

Who names a pile of snow?

Strange people.

With so many of us, and especially almost two dozen Miners and Builders, it took no time at all to gather our agreed upon load of stone blocks and slabs. Since a number of creatures burrowed underground, we didn't want to risk causing cave ins by carrying the far greater weight we actually could have.

By the time we were ready to head back, I found Lydia sprawled on her back, flapping her arms and legs in the snow. Before I could even question her about it, she got up and asked me if I liked her snow angel, pointing at the mark she had left on the ground. The glimmer in her eyes told me she was deliberately trying to confuse me. Still, she swore it was a common thing for humans to do in the snow.

Very strange people.

For the return home, we placed our slabs and blocks of stone over a thicker ice board. We spread out, departing in separate waves, to avoid concentrating the heavy weight of our stones and battle forms. Being stronger in that form, it would make carrying the stones home easier. That also meant there would be no racing this time. From the disappointed expressions on my brothers' faces, I knew racing would become a regular activity among us. I could already think of variations to it with teams and objectives. Xinral gave me the idea earlier when he teamed up with Hyezev to curb Duke's momentum when he tried to overtake them. This would be fun!

Fun. A word we had forgotten for centuries. We used to be a playful people. The Northern Valos would be again.

I sat Lydia on top of my stack of stones blocks and made handles climb the side of the stone from the ice board for her to hang on to if needed. Seeing how we wouldn't move as fast, she probably wouldn't need them.

We hadn't even reached the halfway point when the Valos in the lead veered off course. They waved at us, but I didn't understand their signal. The Hunters closest to me were the first ones to break off, signaling for the others nearby to follow them. I obeyed. Seconds later, I heard a muffled thump and then the first vibration.

Orzarix.

I looked down at Lydia sitting on the stones. Eyes closed, a contented smile stretching her lips, she offered her face to the caress of the sunrays and the cool breeze whipping past us. My stomach twisted with dread. She was too fragile and defenseless. If the beast came after her, she wouldn't stand a chance. Spurred on by fear, I hastened the pace, making the ice board lurch forward.

Startled by the sudden movement, Lydia opened her eyes and cast an inquisitive look toward me. She gripped the ice handles and perked at the louder thump and stronger vibration.

"What was that?" she asked, her head jerking left and right, searching. "Why is everyone scattering?"

"I will keep you safe," I vowed.

As if to challenge that statement, ice and snow exploded a short distance ahead accompanied by the thundering roar of an orzarix. The six massive, deadly white horns on the nightmarish head that came out of the crater marked the beast as an alpha male. Its two front paws emerged from the hole, digging their vicious claws into the frozen ground for purchase. The creature pulled itself up in a shower of ice and snow, then roared again so loudly it hurt. Lydia slapped her hands over her ears and cried out in pain.

The roaring stopped and the beast whipped its head around to look in our direction. Survival on Sonhadra relied heavily on camouflage. My brothers and I, and even the white stones upon which my female sat, blended with this frozen wasteland. Lydia, with her dark skin and red tunic couldn't have made an easier target. The orzarix' yellow eyes locked on her. His mouth stretched in a deadly grin as he bared two rows of lethal teeth and a pair of giant fangs.

Chapter 10

LYDIA

My heart stopped at the sight of the hellish creature. Five or six meters long, the beast resembled a cross between a gorilla and saber-tooth tiger, its mouth full of dagger teeth. Even from the distance, the liquid gold of its eyes hypnotized me. The ice and snow clinging to its long, shaggy white fur went flying as it shook itself like a wet dog. My stomach coiled with terror and the sour taste of fear filled my mouth when it lowered its scale-covered simian head. Six giant horns pointed at me, two on top of its head and the remaining four split in two pairs on each side of its temples like a bull.

It charged at us.

I screamed when strong, cold arms whisked me off the stone blocks and my protector took off running. The spikes and crystalline protrusion along Kai's battle armor dug into my back and behind my legs where he held me. I didn't give a shit. I just wanted us to get the hell away from the monster. Kai ran at lightning speed, the wind whistling in my ears. In spite of that, the pounding of the creature's feet sounded closer. My heart hammered into my throat and my teeth chattered so hard I thought they might break. I didn't know if fear or the brutal jostling of Kai's movements caused it. Needing to see what was happening, I stretched my neck to look over his shoulder.

The other valos raced toward the creature, moving in to intercept. Even in their morphed shape, I could recognize their faces. The Hunters led the counterattack with the Builders close behind. The Crafters stood still at the rear, their hands moving palms up. The gesture summoned spikes and walls of ice in front of the beast. It crashed through them with minimal effort while sustaining no apparent damage. But they slowed it down... at least a little.

Thick ice spears formed in the hands of the Builders which they launched at the monster's face. Like the spikes, they shattered on contact without drawing blood. I couldn't tell if they hurt it or if the splinters stung its eyes, but the creature slowed further, waving one massive paw at incoming projectiles. Blinded, it didn't see the Hunters ram into it in a perfectly coordinated assault. The creature reared back and toppled over from the force of the impact. Hands fisted into giant boulders covered with ice spikes, the valos battered its underbelly. Roaring, no doubt in pain and anger, the beast swiped at its attackers, forcing them to back away so it could roll onto its front.

The Builders resumed pummeling the monster's face with ice spears. While trying to protect its eyes, the creature struggled to get back on its feet. Each time it almost succeeded, one or more Hunter would ram into the supporting legs to force it back down. The whole time, the Crafters battered its underbelly by summoning ice spikes beneath him.

The world stopped shaking when Kai halted at the top of a small hill, one of very few such elevations in the otherwise flat landscape. He put me on my feet and checked me all over for injury.

"I'm fine," I said, craning my neck to look at the action.

Although true, my brain still bounced in my skull from that rocky run, and my skin felt tenderized where Kai's spikes had dug in. A dreadful thought then popped into my mind. He would now leave me to go help the others. My head jerked up toward him as I swallowed down the sour bile of fear.

Reading my thoughts, Kai caressed my cheek to appease me. "Calm, my Lydia. I'm not leaving your side. There are enough of my brothers to handle this without my aid."

I didn't know if he regretted not being able to join them, but relief flooded through me. He drew me into his embrace, my back resting against his chest. Something felt off. It took a moment before it hit me.

"You're not out of breath!"

"No. The valos no longer require air since the change."

Holy cow!

I opened my mouth to ask another question but the enraged roar of the creature demanded my attention. In spite of the terror it inspired me, my heart filled with pity for the creature. It had to be in terrible pain from the beating the valos rained on it. I wished they could end it swiftly.

"Nothing they do seems to harm it," I reflected out loud. "They're only making it angrier."

"They are wearing him down," Kai said.

"Him?" I asked.

"He's an alpha male. A fully mature orzarix, as indicated by the six horns on its head. That fur hides almost impenetrable scales. The only way to kill it is to tire him enough that he runs out of breath. Then, around his neck and nape, three rows of scales will open like the gills of a fish. Those are his vulnerable points."

I shuddered. Had I encountered one of those on my way to the city, it would have eaten me alive. The damn thing was near impossible to kill.

"Are there many of those lurking around?"

Kai's laughter vibrated against my back. "No. They never come near E'Lek. Nothing will eat you, my Lydia."

Thank God for that.

"It will be over soon. There are far too many of my brothers keeping it down. Usually, only three or four Hunters battle them. It can take half a day to defeat an orzarix then."

Kai's words proved prophetic when less than ten minutes later, the fur around the alpha beast's neck rose like frills. Lightning fast, Riaxan's mate—Toerkel I believed he was called—leaped onto the creature's back. His hand extended into a long blade that he jabbed between the *gills*.

The orzarix stilled, a surprised expression on his face. His eyes and face took on a crystalline, icy appearance. His legs shook before his massive body collapsed to the ground, lifting a cloud of snow into the air.

"Clean kill," Kai said, sounding pleased.

"It's still not bleeding," I said, feeling confused, though relieved to be spared the gore.

"It won't," Kai said, picking me up to heading back down the hill. "Toerkel froze his brain. Instant death, no death throes pain."

We rejoined the others and everyone retrieved their stone slabs that had been abandoned here and there for the battle. Four Hunters distributed their stones between their brothers so they could be free to drag the orzarix back to the city. I remembered all too well Kai telling me his people didn't waste. Since they didn't eat, I expected my diet would include a lot of creepy as hell monster steaks in the near future.

IT TOOK FIVE MORE DAYS of stone gathering before the valos felt confident we had enough to try to build the bridge. Kai forbade me to wear colorful outfits anymore when we left the vicinity of the city. White tunics and covering my dark skin with a layer of frost allowed me to blend in with the frozen landscape like the valos did. Thankfully, we didn't encounter another orzarix. I didn't enjoy the scare and it would take me a life time to eat all the meat from the first one.

As predicted, it became part of my daily meal and I experimented with various ways of cooking it. I didn't mind though. It tasted like goat meat. Some curry sauce and naan would have made it even better!

The Crafters and Hunters were still processing every part of the creature, treating its fur taking the brunt of their time.

With the last of the males awakened, those five days gave the valos a chance to grow more accustomed to my presence, and for me to rebuild my strength. Above all, it gave Kai and me the time to bond even more.

I didn't really believe in love at first sight, but I knew something special when it stared me in the face. Whatever was happening between us, I wanted more of it. No one had ever been so sweet and devoted to me. With him, things were simple and honest. I always knew where I stood and how he felt. Although he often found me strange, he accepted our differences and my quirks without qualms. He usually thought them funny or silly, then would end up adopting some of them.

Kai nodded and shrugged like a boss now. I even caught Duke doing it a couple of times.

And the sex...

Holy shit!

Off the chart didn't begin to do it justice. Kai was a machine. I mean, the guy didn't breathe, so no running out of breath or tiring. The best part? I only had to stare at his groin or tickle his navel to get him hard again. Kai proved to be a generous and patient lover, open to experimentation. The first time I went down on him, his heartstone glowed so bright and hot, I feared it would burn right through his back. Teaching him sixty-nine had also been a blast, if somewhat scary with those sharp teeth of his.

For all that, Kai had not been a virgin and knew how to please a woman. When I finally worked up the courage to ask him if he had a girlfriend or mate among their females, he got offended. While very liberal when it came to sex, they didn't cheat when involved in a committed relationship. The valos kept things simple. If you weren't single, you were either paired or mated. Single meant you could sleep with any other single person you wanted, whenever you wanted. Paired could be compared to dating; an exclusive relationship between one—or more—partners, barring all others. And mated constituted a lifetime commitment. Divorce didn't exist among them. According to Kai, we were a pair. To his greatest delight, and relief, I agreed.

That also explained the presence of the bedrooms in the lower-city even though they no longer needed sleep. Before the Creator removed their heartstones, the valos still made use of them to play naughty. When I asked why there were no doors then, Kai explained that when in use, the couple built a wall of ice for privacy and to inform others to keep away.

I wondered how the females would react to my presence.

In a couple of hours, I'd be retrieving their first heartstones if all went well with the bridge. Knowing no scorned ex-girlfriend would try to bash my skull in as a result lessened some of my concerns. However, fear of crossing a lava lake twisted my insides with fear. What if I got stranded on the island? Or worst, what if the bridge collapsed under me? Despite putting up a brave front, Kai shared my worries. But leaving the females to their fate wasn't an option.

After an extra hearty morning meal to pack in energy, I convinced Kai to come bathe with me in the river. He didn't need to bathe. Since I'd never seen him do it, I had inquired as to how he always managed to look so clean and smell so fresh. He explained that he covered his body in a thin sheet of ice, trapping dead skin and dirt within, then shed it, thus cleansing himself in seconds. Still, I relished the thought of sharing my morning routine with him rather than having him sit on the sidelines watching me since the hot spring's water would hurt him.

The rays of the early morning sun shimmered over the snow covered plain, making it shine like a sea of diamonds. Not a single cloud graced the clear blue sky. Since my arrival on Sonhadra two weeks ago, it hadn't rained once although it did snow for a couple of hours. Snow crunched beneath my boot-covered feet as Kai led me by the hand to the river. It was less than fifty meters from the city walls but Kai kept walking further down, past the riverfruit net and beyond a small hill to grant us privacy in case his brothers came out.

I'd found out the riverfruit didn't actually grow in the underground garden as it required a warmer climate. The fruit grew on trees near rivers and lakes and often fell into the water that carried them away toward new grounds in which to take root. A dozen or so made it down the waterfall almost daily, brought down by the current. The net caught them as they floated by the city to be collected by Gatherers. When fed with riverfruit flesh, paexi bugs produced white glowing resin. Kai had therefore been bringing the fruits to the lower-city to continue his work, providing me with much needed sustenance on the day I arrived here.

I shed my tunic and kicked off my boots, enjoying the cold feel of the thick layer of snow beneath my feet. Kai detached his loincloth. His shaft rose proud and tall under my gaze, the slit at the blunt tip winking at me. Although on the impressive side, Kai's rod—as he called it—wasn't scary big. It boasted the same ice blue color as the rest of his skin, with rippling ridges down its length. A single, large ball sac hung beneath it. Aside from the strange braid at the back of their heads, the valos had no body hair. When I suggested shaving my pubic hair, Kai's outraged cry put an end to that. He loved my little curls.

Feeling mischievous, I bent down, raked my hand through the snow, and tossed it at him. Before he could react, I dashed for the river, giggling like a schoolgirl. Within seconds the crunch of his feet pounding the ground caught up to me. A squeal tore out of my throat as his strong arms whisked me off my feet and he continued to barrel down into the river.

Freezing cold water splashed, icy needles pricking my skin and whipping my blood. I loved the cold and didn't expend energy lowering my temperature, knowing my body would adjust naturally. Still laughing, I wrapped my arms and legs around him. Kai's hands settled on my butt, holding me close as he waded in until water licked the bottom curve of my breasts. I'd 'forgotten' the soap and washcloth by my clothes. Something… or rather someone else held my interest at the moment.

We kissed and my inner walls clenched with anticipation. Such ravenous hunger baffled me. I'd had a normal love life before things went to hell. My exes had been nice guys, just not the right ones. The occasional, mostly vanilla sex with lots of foreplay had been my thing. With Kai, the daring, wild, and kinky vixen had taken over. Before, I never would have made the first move. It would have felt... improper, unbecoming. But here, I could give in to my desires and impulses without fear of being judged.

Kai's lips parted and his tongue begged for entry. I welcomed it in. The rough texture caressing and exploring my mouth made my stomach quiver, remembering how it felt between my legs. Mindful of his sharp teeth, our tongues danced together, my mouth tingling from the cold and crisp taste of him.

One of his hands slipped down my butt and between my legs to rub my nub. I moaned in his mouth and pressed myself harder against him. His erection strained against my stomach. How many men could brag about keeping it rock hard in freezing water? Sneaking a hand between us, I wrapped my palm around his length. Kai hissed against my lips and accelerated the movements of his fingers tormenting me. Despite the cold, heat blossomed in the pit of my stomach. I stroked him, the ridges rubbing against my hand reminding me how hollow I felt. Breaking the kiss, I trailed my lips up to the fanned leaf of his ear.

"I need you inside me," I urged.

Too happy to oblige, he let go of my clit and lifted me before impaling me on his erection. I threw my head back, crying out at the fullness. A hungry growl rumbled through Kai's chest vibrating against mine as he rocked in and out of me. My walls tightened at the cold feel of him, enhancing the feel of his ridges with each stroke. Tipping me back, he closed his mouth around my nipple sucking on it with greed. My toes curled with fear and excitement when his teeth grazed the hard nub. Icy water lapped at my spine and my nape, making my skin burn with confusion from the heat building within.

Slipping his hands behind my back on each side of my breasts, Kai bent me even lower onto the surface of the water. Changing the angle of his thrusts, he jerked his hips upward, hitting my sensitive spot each time. Stars exploded behind my eyes. I screamed. Legs shaking and nails digging into his forearms, I surrendered to a chaos of sensations.

Half-dazed, I looked at Kai, towering above me like an ancient god. His bald head blocked the sun's glare, framing him with a bright halo. His wet skin sparkled with the sun's rays and the pulsing light of his heartstone. Eyes glowing, the sharp lines of his face made him even more fearsome as he bared his teeth in pleasure. His hands tightened their hold as he picked up the pace, taking me deeper, faster, harder. I never wanted him to stop.

Water splashed over my stomach and bit at my cheeks. Fear, bliss, and burning need twisted me inside out. My beautiful alien would kill me with pleasure, devour my soul then cast my remains into the frozen depths of the river.

My vision went white and my body seized. The violence of the spasms that rocked my limbs would have sent me under had Kai not pulled me back up against him. Before I could recover, he growled his release in my ear. The heat of his heartstone burned my chest while the icy shards of his seed stabbed my womb. I fell apart again.

Boneless, I collapsed against him, panting on his shoulder. Lost in a sensual haze, I didn't notice Kai carry me to the bank to pick up the cloth and soap, before returning to the river. By the time I'd regained my senses, Kai insisted that he

Unfrozen

finish washing me and I happily let him. Hand in hand, he walked me back to our clothes.

Worry crept back in as my mind shifted to the task that awaited me.

I reached for my white tunic. Two huge obsidian eyes opened in the snow beneath it when I picked it up. The shrill shriek that ripped out of my throat hurt my vocal cords. I recoiled, my hand flying to my chest to keep my heart from pounding its way out. Teeth bared, ready to pounce, Kai took a step forward. He froze when the black eyes blinked and the patch of snow turned out to be a small furry creature. It squeaked, ran off a couple of meters then stopped to face us.

Kai burst out laughing, his stance relaxing. Pulse still racing, I examined the little intruder. The white fur of a Persian cat covered the small, squirrel-like body of the creature. Its fluffy tail perked up behind its head as tiny claws dug into the snow. White scales covered its face which reminded me of a ferret's, except it was wider to accommodate huge black eyes without pupils. It cocked its head and the three rows of ice-blue dragon horns decorating its head glinted under the sun. One started at the tip of its snout and scaled up to the middle of its head in a straight line. The other two began at the forehead and curved towards the ears.

It was freaking adorable!

Which meant it would probably try to eat me, poison me, or lay some crazy alien egg inside my body that would burst out of my chest in a rain of blood and gore. I eyed Kai to know if I should start running, but he just stood there with a silly grin.

The cutie-monster took a couple of steps closer and sniffed the air. Its long claws pierced the snow, leaving small paw prints behind.

"What's it doing? And what is that?" I asked, narrowing my eyes at it.

"She's a sekubu and she's confirming that you're the source of the scent that attracted her here."

I knew it! Never trust the cute ones!

"My scent? She wants to eat me?" I asked, taking a step back.

Kai laughed again and shook his head. "No, my Lydia. Stop fearing things will eat you. You will definitely not be eaten by her, even though sekubus like meat, especially raw. Be careful not to bleed around her."

I gave him the 'so not reassuring me right now' look. He grinned his shark teeth at me.

"Sekubus are usually very shy and skittish, until they find their companion. If you are as kind to her as your scent says you will be, she will adopt you as her caregiver."

My jaw dropped.

Come again?

"*She* adopts *me*, so that *I* can take care of *her*?"

Kai nodded, his expression openly mocking me.

"Shouldn't it be ME *choosing* to adopt her? What if I don't *want* to take care of her?"

I totally wanted to. Even now as she crept closer, I spoke silly, googly words of encouragement to her in my head, like people did when speaking to babies.

He chuckled, putting his loincloth back on. "I'm afraid that is not your decision to make."

Unfrozen

While I put my tunic back on my still damp skin, the little cutie-pie ran up to my feet and licked my big toe. It tickled. I pulled my foot back and she followed. I shook my head at her and reached for my short boots. In a flash of white fur, Cutie ran inside one of them, then poked her head out to stare at me.

"Seriously?"

I picked up the boots but Cutie snuggled in.

"Fine, have it your way," I mumbled with fake annoyance, biting the inside of my cheek, trying not to smile.

Kai grabbed the washcloth and soap then lead me by the hand back to the city. The whole way back, Cutie chirped at me, licking my fingers and occasionally nibbling on them. I almost dropped the boots the first time she flashed the two rows of needle sharp teeth.

"Does everything on this planet have crazy teeth?" I asked, bewildered.

"Yes, my Lydia. Everything but you."

He said it so matter-of-fact, I couldn't even get mad.

As I climbed the first step to the city entrance, Cutie jumped out of my boot, rubbed her temple on my ankle then took off.

"Oh," I said, saddened by her departure.

"She will return," Kai said.

The certainty in his voice dampened my disappointment.

Entering the lower-city gave me an eerie sense of déja-vu aside from the empty alcoves. After two weeks of near constant activity, the absence of a single soul creeped me out. Kai summoned the platform and lowered us to the fourth level where all the valos had congregated. They formed a chain from the chamber where the stone blocks and slabs had been stacked, down the stairs to the entrance of the magma chamber.

I swallowed past the lump in my throat, strings of anxiety knotting in my stomach. Humor had drained from Kai's features, sharpened by tension. All eyes turned to me, the hope shining in them adding even more pressure. The valos parted to let Zak through. He approached me, a pair of thick-soled, knee-high leather boots in his hand. I accepted the gift and put them on, pretending not to understand the possible implication of their length.

Without a word, we climbed down the stairs, the descent oddly cooler than I remembered. Reaching the entrance explained it all. The males had stacked stone blocks along the left side of the path, creating a wall between the lava and us. Five valos in battle form summoned a thick sheet of ice against it to keep it from overheating. It melted in seconds only to be reformed. Down the path, the lava lake still stood between the heartstone altar and us.

"Where's the bridge?" I asked Duke as he handed me a leather bag.

"We were waiting for you to build it. The stones heat up too fast once in direct contact with the lava and start to break."

What?

"They will last long enough for you to return," he amended quickly, seeing my horrified look. "We have tested them to make sure."

That only half reassured me. Kai's hand tightened around mine and a nerve ticked at his temple.

"Okay," I said, thinking the exact opposite.

"We're going to build it now," Duke warned.

I nodded, fighting the nausea roiling in my belly.

The valos came together in a flurry of activity and efficiency. Shifting to their battle form, they passed the stone slabs down the chain. Three Builders—one of them Duke—took turns coming as close to the lava river as possible to push the stone slab into it. Despite their weight, the blocks didn't sink quickly into the lava. The tricky part was each slab only covered half the distance to the island. Once the first slab sank deep enough to be flush with the ground they slid another slab over and past it to bridge the second half connecting to the island. Then they stacked another stone block on the first slab that continued to sink into the lava. Rinse-repeat.

Kai fetched me a small block of stone to sit on then rejoined his brothers laboring through the painstaking process of building the bridge. The speed at which the stone reddened once they came in contact with the lava worried me.

Twenty-eight slabs later, the stones stopped sinking; the bridge was completed. My stomach dropped and my fingers hurt from clenching the leather bag too tight. Kai's gaze connected with mine. Despite the fear he couldn't fully hide, the tenderness and pride in his eyes gave me the strength I needed. He believed in me, counted on me. I wouldn't let him—them—down. Getting up on shaky legs, I kissed him then ran for the bridge. If I tried to walk across at a slower pace, I'd lose all courage and turn tail.

As I cleared the protective wall erected by the valos, the heat that slammed into me took my breath away. The hot air burned my lungs the moment I stepped onto the bridge. It wobbled under my weight and I glanced down at the slow bubbling of the fiery river around me, ready to melt my bones. My stomach lurched. Swallowing my fear, I looked away.

Skin sizzling and eyes stinging, I almost crumbled to my knees once I reached the other side. Had I flared to my highest temperature, this would have been a cakewalk, but I couldn't risk wearing myself out so soon.

I almost cried with relief when I reached the altar and the blessing of its cooling system. But that relief was short-lived. More than fifty heartstones pulsated before me in a large, chandelier-like cluster. Half of them sat out of my reach. I'd forgotten the great height of the Strangers. This wouldn't have been much of a problem for a first round if not for the two flickering heartstones up in the middle of the cluster. From a distance, they had been impossible to notice.

I jerked the arms of the *chandelier* to test its sturdiness. Reassured it could bear my weight, I hoisted myself up. Thank God for small blessings... The perspiration covering my palms and the heavy weight of the heartstones added to the challenge. I couldn't hold myself up and carry more than one of the precious orbs at a time. After retrieving the first one, I climbed down, placed it in the leather pouch then climbed back up. My biceps hurt by the time I got down with the second one. It didn't bode well for carrying the bag afterward.

I shoved another seven heartstones into the pouch, careful not to damage them despite my haste, then picked it up. Its weight made me groan. Turning back towards the bridge, I tried to silence the fear that made my blood rush in my ears. Although the stone slabs still seemed to hold steady, sitting above the line of the lava by the height of a normal step, the reddening edges spelled bad news. Taking a deep breath, I pressed the bag to my chest, and dropped my temperature to the lowest level possible. Once my skin frosted over, I made a dash for it.

An inferno blasted me in the face the instant I left the vicinity of the cluster. My steps faltered and my knees nearly buckled. The heat sat like boulders on my shoulders, weighing me down.

"LYDIA!" Kai's terrified voice spurred me on.

The heartstones didn't allow me to move faster than a brisk walk. By the time I crossed the four meters from the cluster to the edge of the bridge, water squished between my toes from sweat and the frost melting from my skin into my boots. I climbed the short step onto the bridge. The heat choked the air out of me and steam rose from my skin. The frost melted faster than I could regenerate it. I bit back a scream, each breath too precious to waste.

By the fifth step, I discovered a new definition of the word pain.

The burning stone slabs melted the soles of my leather boots, making them sticky, slowing me down further. As I struggled to lift each step, the water accumulating in my boots heated. With no way out, it sizzled and bubbled against my skin. My scream rose at last when steam scraped at my knees. In the distance, Kai shouted my name in a desperate litany. Through the haze, I saw him fight against his brothers holding him back.

The bag began to slip from my strained arms. On instinct, I tightened my hold.

If I drop it, I could flare...

But I couldn't... wouldn't. Pain wouldn't defeat me. If I had survived Dr. Sobin's torture, I would overcome this to save the precious lives in my arms. Plowing through the blistering agony, I put one burning step in front of the next.

I don't recall reaching the other side, only Kai's cold arms embracing me and my burden being lifted from me.

"I didn't drop them," I whispered against his neck. "I didn't drop them."

"No, my Lydia. You didn't."

Chapter 11

KAI

Two days after that horrible rescue mission, Lydia's screams still echoed in my ears. I watched her burn, helpless to assist. When my brothers held me back, I had wanted to kill them, even though they were saving my life.

My Lydia...

Beautiful, strong, and with the most loving heart. Even through the pain she had endured, her thoughts had been for the heartstones. The burns on her skin had been concerning but the ones on her feet and legs from the leather boots devastated me. Zak had kneeled at her bedside begging for forgiveness for the harm his gift had caused her. His intention had been honorable. None of us had accounted for the side effects of her frost. She hadn't blamed him, but still guilt gnawed at him.

With the other Gatherers, he'd gone over the plateau beyond the cliff to fetch tahrija roots to make medicine for her. Once crushed into a fine paste and diluted in water, a single cup sufficed to numb pain. Chewing on a raw piece the size of a yarxin nut would put you to sleep for half a day.

As much as I wanted to see Lydia's eyes and speak to her to make sure she was well, I didn't want her to suffer. The rescue had drained her energy but the pain made her too nauseous to eat. The minute the Gatherers had returned, I'd given her tahrija juice, fed her a little then put her to sleep with a raw piece of tahrija. Boiling the roots made the medicine more potent than crushing it. To my surprise, the heat of the cooking device Lydia called a stove had barely bothered me. Since joining with my female, my tolerance threshold had noticeably increased.

At first, I feared the burns on Lydia's skin would leave permanent scars. It wouldn't have changed my feelings for her, but the sight would remind her of the pain she'd endured. However, after a single day, they had greatly faded. On her legs and feet, the blisters had drained and the scalds had reduced to scabs and reddish patches on her skin.

Last night, no longer feeling pain, Lydia had declined the tahrija juice but agreed to chew on a small piece of the bitter root to help her sleep. Apparently, the scabs on her legs itched so much she wanted to scratch her skin off. I feared the heat had damaged her mind. When I said I wouldn't let her mutilate herself, she laughed and said it was just a human saying.

Strange people.

While she slept, I worked on a surprise for her. After she got hurt, I had carried Lydia directly to the living quarters Duke and the Builders had been preparing for her since it was closest. We'd carved a large bedroom next to the hot spring, with a spacious wardrobe at the back and a hygiene room. The Builders had scavenged some of the parts from the Strangers' dwellings. They'd also built a cooking station in the meeting area near the entrance. I had planned on making it a big reveal once my own work was completed. However, she'd needed to use the hygiene room last night, spoiling those plans.

She'd been moved to tears by it. I didn't understand why extreme happiness made her cry, but as long as joy provoked it, all was well.

Still, she hadn't seen the hot spring; my personal project for her. The sekubu almost gave away that surprise by trying to lure her there. She'd been sneaking into the lower-city multiple times a day looking for my female. I'd even found her sleeping, curled up in a ball, by Lydia's head.

I was hastening through some illumination work when two of the awakened females walked into the room. They stayed at the entrance, indisposed by the heat. Once more, my own absence of discomfort struck me. I'd been working for extended periods without feeling even remotely queasy. However, the warm water from the pool remained unbearable and harmful to me with more than a few seconds of exposure.

I picked up the paexi laying glowing yellowish-brown resin in my carvings—a color which Lydia called amber—and settled it down near a pile of iwaki seeds of that color. It rubbed its black wings together, chirping with contentment. Turning towards the females, I approached them, my cheerful mood dampening at the serious expression on their faces.

"What is it, sisters?" I asked.

I addressed both of them but my eyes rested on Jaankeln, Duke's older sibling. Like him, she had a muscular build and broad shoulders, although she worked as a Miner, not a Builder. Smart and outspoken, she was a natural leader. People often deferred to her. Lorvek, a Crafter female, acted as moderator during conflicts or important debates. That increased my unease.

"We wanted to know how Lydia is faring," Jaankeln said.

"She's on the mend. At the rate she's healing, there should be no scars left in two or three days at the most."

"Hmmm," she said, looking pensive.

I frowned, having expected a different reaction.

"Are you not pleased?" I asked, my tone less friendly.

She gave me an annoyed look.

"Of course, I am pleased. Your female has saved our lives. I understand you are paired?"

I shifted, somewhat uncomfortable by the sudden switch of topic. Lydia and I were indeed paired, even though deep down, I considered her my mate.

"Yes, we are."

And I want much more.

I hadn't known Lydia very long, but I couldn't envision a future without her. She occupied my every thought. Seeing her cross that bridge in agony and thinking I might lose her had made everything clear for me. She was the one—my life mate. I would need to find the right moment to express my feelings and ask if she shared them.

"Congratulations, brother," she said, while Lorvek also whispered a good word. "I hear much about her courage."

"Thank you." I wished they'd just get to the point. "If you wish to see her, I'm afraid you will need to return later. She has eaten some tahrija roots a little while ago."

I ran my hand down my braid, ashamed of the small lie. It had been some time now since she'd eaten it.

"Actually, we're here for you," Jaankeln said. "An informal discussion in the meeting hall has turned into a more serious one. We're all wondering when Lydia will be able to go free the others."

Unfrozen

My spine stiffened and I barely stopped myself from baring my teeth at her.

"Do you, now?" I snarled. "And who is *we?*"

She narrowed her eyes at me while Lorvek frowned.

"Everyone," the Crafter said in a soft voice.

My heartstone flared with anger.

What is going on here?

"You called a meeting with *everyone*, involving *my female* and no one thought of inviting *me?*"

Ice plates formed along my arms, my mass thickening.

"Calm yourself, Qaezul'tek Var E'Lek. There is no need for anger," Jaankeln said in an icy tone that upset me further.

Lorvek placed a hand on her companion's arm to stop her from speaking.

Wise decision.

"No meeting was called," Lorvek said, her tone appeasing. "Like Jaan said, it started as an informal discussion and others joined in. It has since become a formal discussion and so we're here to include you. Time is running out, Qaezul. Riaxan and her child are still trapped below."

"You didn't see it," I ground between my teeth. "My Lydia almost died. She suffered terrible burns."

"That may be, but you admitted yourself that she's almost fully mended," Jaankeln countered.

"But she may not survive another trip!" I spat, my hands fisting spasmodically with rage.

"A risk worth taking," she replied.

I recoiled, speechless for a moment.

"Qaezul—" Lorvek said.

"A risk worth taking?" I asked, ignoring Lorvek.

I took a menacing step towards Jaankeln who lifted her chin defiantly at me.

"Is my mate's life of no value to you?"

"She's not your mate. And while her life does matter," Jaankeln said, not backing down, "more than forty of our sisters, *valos* females, are trapped below."

My jaw dropped, refusing to believe the implication. I cast a glance at Lorvek and my stomach twisted, finding the same grim determination, tinged with sympathy. Storming past them, rage boiling within, I marched to the meeting hall. As per Lorvek's claim, every single Valos stood in attendance. Despite the numerous benches, no one sat.

They watched me approach with varying expressions on their faces: wariness, compassion, shame, and defiance.

"I hear you are all quite eager to put my Lydia's life in danger."

Toerkel, stepped forward.

"None of us wish her ill, and certainly not I. She saved us and we all bore witness to her sacrifice when rescuing our sisters." He took another couple of steps toward me. "My mate and child are trapped below, so I understand how you feel, brother."

"Yet, you would put her in harm's way when she's still covered in burns?"

"No. We only want to know when she can go back," Toerkel said with a tired sigh. "If your mate dies, the remaining females will too."

I flinched. He made a fair point but that didn't lessen my anger.

"It isn't safe!" I snapped. "A few moments more and Lydia would have been trapped on the other side, or burnt to death on that bridge."

"We have made adjustments to make it safer," Duke intervened.

My head snapped toward him. He stood off to my right, thick arms crossed over his chest. His sister Jaankeln by his side. As original message-bearer, she became the focus of my ire.

"Do not eye me with such resentment, Qaezul," she said, her soft tone belying the harshness of her words. "You may find my words offensive, but they are honest. We have a duty to our people."

"Our people? Have we become the Strangers now?"

She recoiled and offended murmurs rose throughout the room.

"They too thought the life of the valos less valuable, expendable," I said.

"It is not the same," she said, waving her hand in a slashing gesture. "The Creator and the Strangers didn't consider us as people at all but merely as tools. We *do not* consider your female as inferior to us. That said, if I had two people before me and could only save one, I admit that the valo would be my choice. It doesn't mean the other person isn't as deserving, if not more. But caring for your own first is natural."

Jaankeln walked up to me and placed a hand on my shoulder.

"However, this situation is different. We're not choosing between two people, but weighing the welfare of a single female against that of forty others. The scale speaks for itself. Had Lydia been born valo, we would still make the same request. As your paired female, she is valo too now."

My heartstone throbbed. I couldn't argue with her reasoning. The rational part of me agreed, had known all along.

"I will do it," Lydia said.

All heads jerked toward the entrance of the meeting hall. Lydia stood, leaning against the wall, the angry red and discolored patches of skin along her legs plain to see. Additional scabs had healed during her rest cycle. Cutie, huddled at her feet, chirped in greeting.

"I just need a couple of days more to heal."

"Lydia," I said, walking towards her.

She cupped my face in her hands once I reached her.

"They are right, Kai. My people have a saying for that. The needs of the many outweigh the needs of the few."

Too choked for words, I drew her into my embrace and held her tight.

"We thank you, for your understanding, sister," Jaankeln said.

I picked up Lydia in my arms and carried her to the dwelling in the upper-city, away from them, away from this.

THE NEXT TWO DAYS WENT by too fast. Lydia had fully recovered, thanks to whatever strange healing property the evil scientist had given her during the experiment.

Her legendary appetite had returned and she gorged on orzarix meat to rebuild her strength. The Gatherers had gone out of their way, scouring the frozen plains, going even as far as the plateau beyond the waterfall to fetch new produce for Lydia. It would be some time before the crops grew. It gave them both purpose and an opportunity to express their gratitude to my female. She took a particular liking to the thick juices made of various crushed fruits the Gatherers prepared. Her people had something similar, although of different flavors, which they called smoothie.

Cutie no longer left Lydia's side, making a nuisance of herself when she felt my female neglected her in my favor. The annoying creature made it a point of reminding us of her presence during our moments of intimacy. When I locked her out of the room, she would whine and keen without end. Lydia found it endearing.

Strange female.

I had wanted to delay the inevitable by a few more days but quite a few heartstones had dimmed. Plus, the sooner we got this out of the way, the better for all concerned.

We headed to the magma room where my brothers... our brothers had the bridge almost completed. Zak had crafted sandals with thick leather soles for Lydia, with stone rivets beneath it to keep the leather from direct contact with the heated bridge. It would reduce the risks of the leather melting and sticking to it, yet keeping it flexible enough to allow a normal walk.

Lydia practiced walking in them while we waited for the bridge to be done. The Crafters had also made a ladder for her in kumeri wood. Light, but extremely resilient, it would allow her to reach the heartstones located higher in the cluster without problem.

My brothers had built a bridge twice the width of the previous one so the surface heat from the lava lake wouldn't affect her as much. They had also cut thinner slabs of stone to put atop the thicker ones below once she was ready to return in case the bridge had already overheated. When I expressed concerns how they would get them on top, they said an ice ramp would last long enough to allow the slabs to slide over. Once in contact with the lava, the ice that didn't evaporate would form solid bubbles around the platform.

I wasn't quite reassured by this but we were committed.

With one last kiss, I let my beloved go. She shoved her sandals into the leather bag for the heartstones and grabbed the ladder in her other hand. Barefoot, she ran across the bridge, flaring up so the heat didn't crush her like last time. In seconds, she had propped the ladder up, put her sandals on, and was picking up the heartstones.

It looked effortless... almost too easy.

My chest burned with the pulsing glow of my chaotic emotions. Fear and hope warred for control as Lydia headed back over the bridge, skin frosted and the heavy bag held in her tight embrace. The top slab of the bridge had barely even started to redden. Zak's sandals worked beyond my expectations. Thanks to the rivets, she didn't have to battle the sandals sticking to the bridge and crossed back with minimal discomfort.

I almost roared with joy and relief when she hopped off the bridge unscathed. Besides the slight reddening of her skin and the strain of the heavy bag, Lydia appeared fine. But when our eyes met, my stomach knotted and my smile faded. She didn't need to speak for me to know she intended to go back. One look at my brothers revealed they hoped she would. As Toerkel relieved her of the precious bag, Duke approached her holding an empty one. He neither spoke nor gestured for her to take it, leaving the choice up to her. Without a word, she grabbed it.

A dull pain radiated in my chest. Yet, when our eyes met again, I silenced my fears and smiled in encouragement. As much as I wanted to drag her away to safety, Lydia wouldn't be deterred from this course of action and needed my support to see it through. Had she not been my mate, I too would have wanted her to continue.

She pressed her lips to mine. My arms ached with the desire to wrap around her and never let go. Pulling away, she removed her sandals, flared and ran back across the bridge. The burning sensation in my chest expanded as I watched my mate picking the heartstones with haste, willing her to return.

A cold hand settled on my shoulder.

Jaankeln.

"I see now why you care so deeply for her," she said in a soft voice. "You are blessed to have found such a worthy mate. Her presence honors us."

A heartfelt compliment coming from her.

I nodded in acknowledgment, my throat too constricted by worry and emotion to speak. She squeezed my shoulder then went to replace one of the valos icing the protective wall so he could take a break from the heat.

Lydia turned back to the bridge. I perked up, my gaze flying to the stone surface. It looked a little less red than the first time she had tried a few days ago, when the boots had scalded her legs. Once again, the rivets served their purpose. However, the increased heat from the bridge melted her frost too fast and steam rose in steady streams from her skin. Her face contorted with pain but she trudged on. As soon as she cleared the bridge, I moved forward, meeting her halfway.

I relieved her of the bag, passing it blindly behind me to one of my brothers. She radiated heat and had reddened further, but showed no signs of blisters or burns. Despite the discomfort, I held her tight and crushed her lips. She returned the kiss then pushed me back.

The look in her eyes terrified me.

"Lydia?" I asked, shards of dread clawing down my back.

She swallowed hard then averted her eyes, seeking Duke.

"I need a big bowl of that thick fruit juice, right now, and another bag."

Duke turned around and raced up the stairs without a word.

"NO!" I grabbed her shoulders and forced her to look at me. "I forbid it! You are in no condition to go back. The bridge is falling apart. You are safe. Unharmed. We'll build another bridge in a few days. You—"

"Stop, Kai. STOP!"

My mind reeled with fear, confusion, and anger. Why would she want to go back now?

Unfrozen

She cupped my face with both hands, her thumbs caressing my cheeks.

"They don't have a few days. If I don't get them out right now, they will all be dead before morning."

I opened my mouth to argue but she pressed one of her thumbs on my lips.

"Shhh... Listen to me, my love," she said, her voice soft but urgent. "Every time I remove a heartstone, the cooling system attached to its holder stops functioning. This is why the room has been steadily warming up since I started these rescue missions. The heat on the island is rising. It's barely tolerable anymore. There is no other choice."

"I can't lose you, my Lydia." My voice choked on her name.

"And you won't," she said. "You are the best thing that has ever happened to me. I never thought anyone could make me as happy as you do. My heart beats for you."

My heartstone flared, this time with love for my female. Joy and fear battled for dominance.

"You are everything to me, my Lydia. No other can make me complete but you. I want you to be my life mate."

I hadn't meant to blurt out those words, not here, not like this, but I could no longer contain my feelings.

She beamed at me, her eyes filled with such love it melted my insides and warmed the ice in my veins.

"Yes," she whispered. "A million times yes."

Duke appearing at the edge of my vision shattered my happiness. Lydia caressed my cheek and kissed my lips before taking the large jug of smoothie from him. She drank it down, sparing no time to breathe. I cast a glance at the bridge. Although only moments had gone by, its color terrified me.

Lydia handed the empty jug back to Duke and took the bag. "Once I'm across, put those thinner slabs on top so I can return," she told him.

"They won't last for two trips, sister," Duke warned.

"I don't have the strength for two more. I'll bring all the remaining heartstones with this trip," Lydia said. "There's thirteen remaining. Lucky number. It will be heavy but I can do it."

"Lucky number?" I asked.

She snorted and kissed my lips. "A human thing."

Bending down, she removed her sandals.

"Return to me, my Lydia," I begged.

"I swear it."

She flared and ran back over the bridge, taking my soul with her.

Chapter 12

LYDIA

As soon as I dropped my flare, heat came crashing down all around me. The cooling system of the altar barely offered any reprieve. The heartstones cradled on it were dimming at an alarming rate. I had told Kai they wouldn't last the night, but now it was clear they wouldn't last an hour. Although I'd give anything to be back in the safety of his arms, seeing this confirmed I'd made the right decision.

After shoving my feet in the sandals, I reached for the remaining heartstones, all located at the bottom of the altar. I tossed them into the bag in a hurry while taking care not to damage them. A loud hiss resonated behind me. Startled, I nearly dropped the heartstone in my hand and turned around. Steam bellowed around the bridge as a thin slab of stone settled on top. The ice that didn't evaporate bubbled over its edges and appeared to solidify. Turning back to the altar, I grabbed the last three orbs and closed the leather bag.

I took a deep, steadying breath and immediately regretted it. It burned my lungs and made me cough. Lifting up the bag, my arms and lower back complained about its weight. The two previous trips had taken a toll and the extra heartstones for this final trip made matters worse. A whimper escaped my throat when my skin frosted. The room temperature felt like a furnace. By the time I crossed the short distance to the bridge, my forearms already shook from the effort and my skin sizzled with my frost evaporating.

Only sixteen meters to go and this is over.

So close, yet much too far away. The most important were the ten meters of the bridge. Even if I collapsed on the other side, the valos could cross the remaining six meters unprotected by their artificial wall. They would suffer a great deal but wouldn't die.

I stepped onto the bridge. My stomach lurched when it wobbled beneath my feet. The supporting stones below were disintegrating from the heat. Time was running out. Fighting the fatigue in my legs, I took two more steps forward.

A pop, a hiss, and an inferno engulfed me.

Scalding steam blew across my legs and left arm as one of the steam bubbles from the ice burst open from the pressure of my weight on the slab. I screamed, stumbling back. The movement popped a couple more bubbles on my right side. My vision darkened and the ground rushed toward me.

I hit the bridge hard and rolled off. By some miracle, I landed back onto the island. In the distance, Kai's voice calling me kept me from surrendering to oblivion. If I lost consciousness now, I'd never rise again. Wanting to sit up, I rolled to my side and cried out as the hard surface of the island pressed against my blisters. A series of pops and hisses made me look up. Kai and a few valos were launching ice shards at the remaining bubbles.

As I struggled to my feet, it struck me that the temperature had lessened as had my pain.

I had flared up.

Shit!

This would hurt the heartstones!

My dying will hurt the heartstones more.

Unfrozen

"LYDIA!" Kai shouted.

My gaze, blurred by the heat and pain, snapped up in his direction. With a will of their own, my feet moved forward. I maintained the flare, my heart breaking for the precious package in my arms. Latching on to Kai's voice, he became my beacon, leading me home one step after the other. I ignored the wobbling of the platform beneath me, the smell of burnt skin, and the debilitating pain that threatened to bring me to my knees.

I'm coming back to you, Kai. I'm coming back to you.

I don't recall stepping off the bridge or handing over the bag. A wall of ice surrounded me and Kai's voice whispered in my ear.

"I've got you, my Lydia. You're safe."

I smiled through the pain and gave in to the darkness.

MY BURNS HAD BEEN SEVERE. I didn't know enough of the medical jargon to say if it was second or third degree. Either way, Kai had taken me straight to the river to release the heat my burns kept trapped inside my body. I'd been coming in and out of consciousness for three days. He'd immediately dose me with more tahrija juice then made me chew a small piece of the root to knock me out.

I welcomed it.

On the fourth day, Kai denied me the root. He knew I was hiding from my memories, from facing the fate of those last thirteen females whose heartstones had burned in my arms.

Or so I thought.

I didn't save them all, but eleven made it, far more than I had imagined. Both deceased females had been mated but one of their males had died in hibernation years ago. The other male was devastated. Although he mourned his mate, he apparently didn't blame me, or so Kai swore. Riaxan and her baby both survived and thrived. They'd been part of the second run I'd made. She and Toerkel wanted to introduce their infant son to me once I'd recovered enough.

Kai held me as I fell apart in his arms with relief for the survivors and sorrow for the lost. Physical contact hurt too much on my burns though, so he had let go. Unlike my previous injuries, these would take at least a couple of weeks to mend.

Kai too had been injured. It turned out I'd only made a few steps after getting off the bridge before I collapsed three meters from the protective wall. Kai had caught me and sustained some serious damage from both the excessive heat in the room and from my body still hot from flaring. And yet, only dark blue patches marred his muscular chest and arms.

Since the change, valos healed most injuries to their battle form in hours, but took weeks to mend those sustained by their regular form. Kai had taken days. With the increased resistance to heat he'd noticed, we believed I'd passed some of Quinn's healing abilities to him as well as some of my heating powers during our moments of intimacy. He seemed to have affected me as well since my frost reached even lower levels than before. I wondered if he would pass other traits to me such as his long life.

That'd be awesome!

It took three weeks for me to fully recover and the last of my scars to fade. Three weeks during which my heart filled with even more love for my valo. Kai nursed me back to health, bathing, feeding, and entertaining me. He took particular pleasure fixing my hair, its texture fascinating him. As an artist, he would go crazy making up fancy hairdos weaving in gems, flowers and ribbons. Cutie would go wild, pawing at them until Kai chased her off, only to sneak back in and mess with his work again.

At night, we sat on the terrace on the roof and watched the Northern Lights shimmer over E'Lek. He would tell me about his people and life before the Creator. I would shower him with tales of Earth and the *strange* humans. Our wedding ceremonies held a particular interest to him. I didn't need to ask why. In my mind, we were already married in all the ways that mattered. Nevertheless, it made me warm and fuzzy inside knowing he wanted to claim me before his people as his life mate.

We would officially tie the knot in the morning. Jaan refused to let me see my own wedding gown until then. Duke's sister had become my best friend after I barely survived that last rescue. Cutie didn't seem to mind, which confused me considering how she constantly got in the way with Kai. Turns out, she wasn't jealous of the attention I bestowed on Kai but on the attention he bestowed on me. The brat wanted some valo TLC of her own.

When bedtime came around, Kai didn't argue when I said he couldn't spend the night with me, as per human tradition. His cooperation should have pleased me but it didn't. A silly—okay fine, needy—part of me wished he had argued, begged, and pleaded. Instead, I snuggled with Cutie in my giant bed while Kai rejoined his brothers.

Sleep claimed me the instant my head hit the pillow.

Whatever happened to prenuptial jitters and cold feet?

Even Cutie's usual nibbling on my toes didn't wake me. It still baffled me that she hadn't made me bleed yet with those needle sharp teeth of hers. Then again, Kai hadn't cut me either with his shark teeth despite all our tongue wrestling.

Jaankeln and Riaxan had the pleasure of stirring me from that restful sleep. To my surprise, the morning was already quite advanced, with noon barely a couple of hours away. They ushered me to the roman pool inside my dwelling while they laid out my outfit in the living area. I bathed with baby Teo whose default body temperature was closer to a human's and who required food and sleep like me. Teo teemed with life and energy. Barely six months old, sharp little teeth already poked out of his gummy grins.

The valos were excited at the prospect of more children. Whether Kai and I could have any of our own remained a mystery, but I kept my fingers crossed.

After drying off and handing Teo over to his mother, Jaan sat me down in the living area and offered me a simple breakfast made of a thick smoothie and a bar made of crunchy nuts, dried fruits, and cereals. Apparently, there would be a proper wedding feast so I couldn't stuff my face too much. They'd covered the windows overlooking the plaza to keep me from peeping.

During my humble meal, the Valo females trickled into the house, decked out with jewelry and shimmering loincloths. Flat-chested like their males, they didn't wear tops, only multi-row necklaces of beads, polished stones and gems.

This gathering was their version of a bachelorette party, but focused on telling raunchy stories meant to embarrass the bride, or funny cautionary tales about mated life. Thankfully, the spacious living area could accommodate them, even though things got a little tight.

Unfrozen

When Lorvek walked in with a basket full of bugs, Jaan had to hold me down on the bench so I didn't run away screaming. The paexi looked like black-winged snails with the heads of a praying mantis. Despite resembling a shell, the bump on their back was actually a sack filling up with glowing resin colored according to what they ate.

Lorvek propped my feet up and drew patterns on them with a sticky pink gel which she also applied to my toenails. She then set the paexi on them to have a party. I couldn't decide whether tickled and amazed superseded grossed and freaked the fuck out. The critters ate the pink gel and left a glowing white trail in their wake. It looked incredible against my dark skin. However, no matter how pretty this was, I had bug vomit or poop illuminating me.

Did I say gross?

At least, Cutie didn't try to eat them. She was too busy getting petted by all the women in the large attendance anyway.

Lorvek repeated the process on the back of my hands while Riaxan got busy with my hair. She split it into a dozen braids, weaving a glowing ribbon into two of them, then wrapped them in an elaborate bun at the back of my head. She pinned it with an ivory, jeweled comb.

"Something old," Riaxan said with a shy smile. "It belonged to my mother."

My throat tightened and my eyes stung. Even that my beautiful Kai had remembered.

As soon as Lorvek had removed the creepy crawlers off of me, Jaan approached with the dress.

"Something new," she said, holding it up before me.

It took my breath away.

Kai had grilled me with questions about wedding gowns, but this would put the greatest couture houses to shame. Jaan helped me slip it on. Ice blue shimmering fabric, the color of my eyes, draped into a Grecian dress. The plunging neck hinted at the curve of my breasts. The plated, layered skirt flowed around me, fanning out in a long train. Luminous highlights glowed along the plating like the rays of the sun had been captured in the folds, and ornate swirls decorated the hem.

Lorvek clasped two armbands, one on each of my bare arms, made from the ivory horns of the orzarix the Hunters defeated while retrieving the stones. An iwaki flower had been carved on it, its outline illuminated, and precious gems inserted along its petals.

"Something borrowed," Lorvek said, tying a choker around my neck, covered in glowing tribal patterns and white, blue and purple gems. "A gift from my life mate," she explained.

The laughter and chatter of the women died down when Jaan made me sit again and placed a delicate tiara on my head, with more stylized iwaki flowers around a large, ocean-blue gemstone.

"Something blue," she said.

The weight of nearly fifty pair of eyes settled on my shoulders. The females sat in a half circle around me, some on the couches, others directly on the floor, a few stood along the back wall.

"Thank you for letting us share your special day and tradition," Lorvek said, followed by approving murmurs from the other females. "And thank you for saving all of us. We hope this day will mark the beginning of a very happy life for you with us, your new family."

Unfrozen

One by one, they took turns hugging me. Blinking away the tears pricking my eyes, I returned their embraces. It was more than just gratitude for their acceptance that moved me. Until this moment, I had still feared I might not receive full acceptance from the valos.

"It is time to join your mate," Riaxan said.

Lorvek checked that the illumination on my skin had sufficiently dried before slipping a pair of white sandals on my feet with the same gems and highlights as the rest of my outfit. I didn't know what material it was although it felt like leather.

A silly thought crossed my mind. The way I glowed all over, I'd make a pretty fancy white and blue Christmas tree!

They led me out of the house in a procession. The valos had reclaimed the city, cleaning it up, reopening the dwellings and removing all the faces of the Strangers carved on buildings, especially any representations of Tarakheen. The statues they hadn't taken down, they had remodeled to resemble the Northern Valos.

Duke waited for me outside, barefoot, wearing nothing but a loincloth. To my surprise, his was black with silver highlights. The females had all come in pale colored, shimmering loincloths ranging from ice blue to pinks and pale yellows. They headed down towards the plaza while I approached him.

He extended a bouquet of frozen, exotic flowers in shades of lavender, white, pale blue, and a hint of pink. Swallowing past the lump in my throat, I accepted the flowers and hooked my arm around his. As my matron of honor, Jaan stood in front of us before heading down the main path toward the plaza. Duke led me down the aisle in her wake.

On both sides of the path, ice flowers appeared with each of my steps. I couldn't say which valo was creating them, but it was beautiful.

Up ahead, Roman columns made of snow separated the rows of ornate benches on each side of the aisle where the valos had congregated. Snow sculptures representing floral arrangements bordered the pathway. A clever play with glow stones added the perfect touch of color and glitter. A flowery scent even permeated the plaza. How they had achieved that left me baffled.

But for all its beauty, this winter wonderland, fairy tale setting didn't hold my attention. At the end of the aisle on an elevated stone dais, Kai stood waiting for me. Looking at my soon to be husband, my pulse raced and my skin heated. Barefoot, he also wore a black loincloth with ornate silver trims and jeweled beads. A shoulder mantle of black leather left his muscular chest and heartstone exposed. It reminded me of the old roman gladiator armor.

Eyes locked with my intended, I glided down the aisle in a dream-like state. Climbing the three steps up the dais after Jaan, my knees wobbled in sync with the thrumming of my heart. She turned around to face Kai and me but I only had eyes for my man. Duke said something, I think the whole deal about giving away the bride. It was all noise to my ears. Kai's heartstone shone so bright with emotion, the heat radiated against my skin. His cold hands grabbed both of mine and I drowned in the icy depth of his eyes.

The valos didn't have religion as we did. No priest officiated weddings and they didn't make all this frilly stuff for it either. Before the change, the couples would exchange their vows in private, announce it to the tribe, and a big potluck would be organized followed by games to celebrate. That they'd gone to such lengths for me moved me to the core.

Although she addressed me, Jaan projected loud enough for all in attendance to hear.

"You have come to Sonhadra, fallen from the sky," she said, her voice solemn. "Fate has led your steps to E'Lek. Through courage and sacrifice, you have given us life again and saved our people from extinction."

My heart constricted and my vision blurred with tears. Kai's hands tightened around mine.

"We are all here because you put your life at risk to save complete strangers," Jaan said under the agreeing whispers of the assembly. "You owed us nothing, yet gave us everything. The first visitors from the sky destroyed our world and you rebuilt it. We are here today to welcome you as our true sister, not only because you are mating our brother Qaezul, but because you have earned a special place in our hearts. You are valo."

"You are valo," the others repeated in unison.

The dam broke and I bawled and sniffled to a mix of amused chuckles and fake indignation about crying on my mating day. Kai held me and kissed the tears away from my cheeks until I regained my composure. My cheeks burned from having made such a spectacle of myself.

"Lydia," Jaan asked, "do you take this male as your life mate, for better or for worse, until death do you part?"

"I do." My words came out whispered, my throat almost too constricted to breathe.

This line also wasn't part of the valos traditions, but adapted just for me.

"Qaezul, do you take this female as your life mate, for better or for worse, until death do you part?"

"I do," he said, his voice shaking with emotion.

"You may now seal your bond with blood," Jaan said.

The valos didn't exchange rings but mixed their blood in a blood oath. Extending his finger into a sharp icy blade, Kai made a small incision in his palm. I presented him with my right hand and he made a small cut there for me. Although it should have scared me, I raised my uninjured hand to my collar and parted the left pane of my dress to expose my heart. Kai made a cut and immediately covered it with his bleeding palm. At the same time, he grabbed my wounded hand and brought it to his heartstone. Its glass-like shield parted to receive my blood then closed again.

A tingling sensation spread through me from both the incision in my hand and on my chest. Electric shocks coursed through my body. For a moment, my vision blurred and my head swam. Kai blinked and looked somewhat unsteady on his feet, appearing to have been as affected as I. The zapping faded but a strange, yet pleasant warmth lingered.

"I declare you husband and wife," Jaan said, "life mates before all of Sonhadra. You may kiss the bride."

Cheers erupted all around us and snowflakes created by the valos fell over the dais as Kai's lips pressed against mine.

Epilogue

LYDIA

After the wedding, since none of them ate, the valos held a feast for one—me—at the entrance of the city. I enjoyed it while watching a show of death racing. Nobody died, obviously, but they went out of their way to knock out their rivals, erecting ice walls in their path or deliberately bumping into each other. I almost choked a few times laughing myself to tears.

They had set the table at the foot of the giant statue of Tarakheen at the entrance of the city. To my shock, they had reshaped her to my likeness. Although flattered and deeply touched, E'Lek didn't belong to me and I didn't want them thinking in any way that I held such ambitions. Both Jaan and Lorvek reassured me none of them believed that. Kai had carved iwaki flowers at my feet and in my cupped palms which stretched outwards in an offering gesture.

To the Northern Valos, I was Lydiazul'vir Dor E'Lek, the Giver of Life.

Two days later, the Builders and Crafters completed the funeral chamber for their brothers and sisters who hadn't survived the magma room. They used the room where the females had been enshrined and other Artisans joined their efforts to Kai's to make it bright and beautiful with colorful carvings. The valos didn't decay upon death. They froze, their bodies remaining in a permanent stasis. Walking inside, you could almost think you'd entered a wax museum.

In the weeks that followed, we held many discussions as to the future of E'Lek. Although the Northern Valos had kept minimal contacts with the other valo cities, they had relied heavily on trade with the City of Light. They intended to resume their business with them, assuming they were still a thriving people. The Crafters would visit them the next time they returned.

I still struggled to wrap my head around the fact that a valo city had been built on top of a giant dinosaur. Apparently, the Creator of the City of light had bioengineered three of those beasts. They were so heavy the ground shook for miles around with each of their steps. I realized now it was what had awakened me after I'd washed up on the bank of the frozen land. It came by once every month. Kai promised to take me there once the Hunters made sure it was safe. I could hardly wait.

I wondered if potential survivors of the *Concord* had encountered any of those other valos. A few weeks ago, the Hunters had found the half-eaten remains of one of the prisoners, recognizable by his orange outfit. No one else had made it this close to E'Lek. I still had mixed feelings about it. Part of me would welcome the presence of another human, but I trusted very few of them. Once the Hunters made contact with the other cities, we'd know for sure. They promised to inquire about my girls; Quinn, Zoya and Petra. It would be wonderful to see them again. Maybe I could hook them up with one of the guys here. Duke was a good sort.

We also wondered about the lost tribes. The majority of the valos here were born or married in E'Lek. We had no idea what the Creator had done to the four nomadic tribes of the Northern Valos before anyone realized what was happening. They could be somewhere out there, wasting away in hibernation too. A few Hunters and Miners had set out to try and discover what had befallen them and if they could be rescued.

With the valos having reclaimed the upper-city, the lower-city still served as a workplace for growing the crops and crafting. The suite Kai and Duke had built there for me also served as a romantic getaway. With much effort and ingenuity, my mate had managed to keep his surprise a secret. On our wedding day, Kai had revealed the breathtaking work he had done in the hot spring room of the lower-city.

Originally, it had been a dimly lit room with a rough-edged pool and uneven stone walls. Now, a giant fresco of me sitting in a field of iwakis with Cutie on my lap decorated the entire back wall. The side walls displayed various scenes related to the life of his people before the change. Glow stones embedded in strategic places on the floor and ceiling bathed the room in a soft, intimate glow. Touchstones on intricately ornate pedestals in the corner of the room could be activated for more light. But it was the ceiling that took my breath away making Michelangelo's Sistine Chapel look like amateur work.

When I asked him how he'd managed to do this in the heat of the room, he explained that he'd been able to tolerate more of it since we'd become intimate. Two months after our wedding, any doubts we held that we affected each other had evaporated. While he still couldn't withstand serious heat like in the magma room, Kai's default body temperature now loomed closer to a human's. Best part, he could also handle the heat of the hot spring's water for extended periods without sustaining any damage. Something happened the day we exchanged blood and I couldn't be happier.

I sat naked at the edge of the pool, feet dangling in the water. Kai jumped in from the opposite side and swam up to me. Standing between my parted legs, he lifted his head to kiss me. I cupped his face in my hands and kissed him back with all the love that bubbled in my heart for him.

"I have a secret to tell you," I whispered against his lips.

"What is it, my Lydia?"

I grabbed his hand and placed it on my stomach. He stiffened then his eyes widened, the question obvious on his face. I nodded in response.

"Looks like little Teo will soon have a friend to play with," I said.

His heartstone shone bright, his face contorted with emotion.

"My Lydia… My iwaki…"

I smiled and kissed my husband again.

THE END

Valos of Sonhadra

THE VALOS OF SONHADRA series is the shared vision of nine sci-fi and fantasy romance authors. Each book is a standalone, containing its own Happy Ever After, and can be read in any order.

Amanda Milo - Alluvial

Poppy Rhys - Tempest

Nancey Cummings - Blazing

Ripley Proserpina - Whirlwind

Naomi Lucas - Radiant

Isabel Wroth - Shadowed

Tiffany Roberts - Undying

Marina Simcoe - Enduring

Regine Abel - Unfrozen

Other Books

Thank you for reading!
If you enjoyed my work, please check out my other novels and keep your eyes peeled for upcoming releases.

THE VEREDIAN CHRONICLES SERIES
Raising Amalia
Escaping Fate
Losing Amalia
Blind Fate

DARK TALES
Bluebeard's Curse
Anton's Grace

THE SHADOW REALMS
Dark Swan

VALOS OF SONHADRA
Unfrozen

Follow Me

I'D LOVE TO HEAR FROM you! If you want to comment on my books, find out what I'm up to or just want to chat, don't be shy and come say hello:

LINKS

https://www.regineabel.com/

https://www.facebook.com/regine.abel.author/

https://twitter.com/regineabel

https://www.bookbub.com/profile/regine-abel

https://smarturl.it/RA_Newsletter

ABOUT THE AUTHOR

Regine Abel is a fantasy, paranormal and sci-fi junky. Anything with a bit of magic, a touch of the unusual and definitely a lot of romance, will have her jumping for joy. Hot alien warriors meeting no-nonsense, kick-ass heroine give her warm fuzzies. Through her Veredian Chronicles series, Regine will take you to an exciting alien world full of mystery, action, passion and new beginnings. Follow Amalia and her Veredian sisters – enslaved, exploited and hunted – as they fight for their freedom and the right to love. In her Dark Tales series, Regine will make you rediscover the fairy tales of your youth in a sexy, dark, and twisted reimagining of the classics.

When not writing or reading, Regine surrenders to the other passion in her life: video games! As a professional Game Designer and Creative Director, her career has led her from her home in Canada to the US and various countries in Europe and Asia.

Printed in Poland
by Amazon Fulfillment
Poland Sp. z o.o., Wrocław